## THE WIZARD'S SPELL

Garth snatched up his sword and faced the wizard again.

"Overman," Shang said, his voice hoarse with pain and hatred, "I *had* meant your death to be quick and painless. But now you will die slowly."

Garth made no reply, but approached the crippled and unarmed wizard with raised sword. He never reached him.

Shang made a curious gesture, and the overman froze in midstride. Despite his mental struggle, his sword began to descend, his legs to sag. He dropped numbly to the flagstone floor.

Shang stared at Garth, his eyes glittering. "The Cold Death is slow, overman. Do not bother to struggle; you will only hasten the end by tiring yourself. Nothing can break the spell while I live."

By Lawrence Watt-Evans
Published by Ballantine Books:

## THE LORDS OF DÛS

Book One:
The Lure of the Basilisk

Book Two:
The Seven Altars of Dûsarra

Book Three:
The Sword of Bheleu

Book Four:
The Book of Silence

**The Cyborg and the Sorcerers**

**The Misenchanted Sword**

# The
# LURE
## of the
# BASILISK

Book One of *The Lords of Dûs*

*Lawrence Watt-Evans*

A Del Rey Book

BALLANTINE BOOKS • NEW YORK

A Del Rey Book
Published by Ballantine Books

Library of Congress Catalog Card Number: 79-55014

ISBN 0-345-33466-3

Printed in Canada

First Edition: March 1980
Fourth Printing: November 1985

Map by Chris Barbieri

Cover art by Darrell K. Sweet

Dedicated to
Moshe Feder,
the first editor
to tell me I
could write

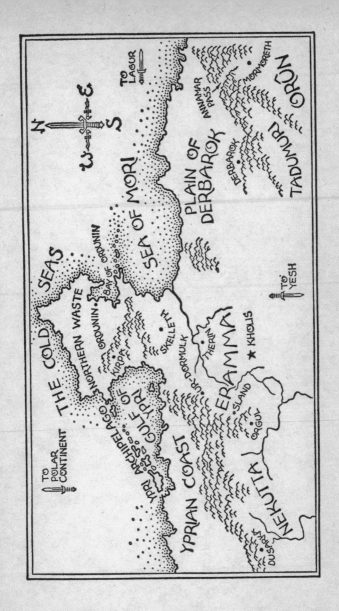

# PROLOGUE

"I am weary of all this death and dying."

The speaker was a huge armor-clad figure almost seven feet in height, standing at the narrow mouth of a small cave near the top of a snowy and rubble-strewn hillside. Even from a distance an observer would have seen the fading light of the setting sun glinting a baleful red from his eyes, marking him as something other than human. He was speaking to a bent, crouching creature clad in tatters who stood inside the cave's mouth, at the edge of the impenetrable gloom of the interior, her face and form only faintly visible in the dim twilight. She was hunched and humpbacked, shriveled and bent with age. Her face was twisted and broken, her teeth gone, one of her golden eyes squinted horribly, yet she was plainly of the same race as the tall warrior.

"Death is everywhere," the decrepit creature replied.

"I know that, Ao; I would it were not so." The hag addressed as Ao merely shrugged, and the warrior continued: "It makes life pointless—to know that I and all I know will die and pass away, as if I had never been." He paused briefly, then went on. "I wish that it were possible for me to perform some feat of cosmic significance, to change the nature of things, so that all would look back millennia from now and say, 'Garth did this.' I wish that I could alter the

1

uncaring universe so that even the stars would respond to my passing, so that my life would not be insignificant."

Ao moved uncomfortably. "You are a lord and a warrior whose deeds will be recalled for a generation."

"I am known to a tiny corner of a single continent; and even there, as you yourself say, I will be remembered only for a century or two, an instant in the life of the world."

"What would you have of us, my sister and myself?"

"Is it possible for a mortal being to alter the way things are?"

"That, it is said, is the province of the gods; if the gods are the baseless myth some believe them, then it is the role of Fate and Chance."

Garth had apparently expected this reply; there was only the slightest pause before he said, "I would have it, then, that if I cannot change the world, at the least the world shall remember me. I would have it that my name shall be known as long as anything shall live, to the end of time. Can this be?" He stared at the misshapen hag, his usually expressionless face intent.

She gazed back impassively and answered slowly, "It is your desire that you be known throughout history, from now until the end of the world?"

"Yes."

"This can be done." Her tone seemed curiously reluctant.

"How?"

"Go to the village called Skelleth, and seek there the Forgotten King; submit yourself to him, obey him without fail, and what you have wished will be."

"How am I to find this king?"

"He is to be found in the King's Inn, clad in yellow rags."

"How long must I serve him?"

Ao drew a deep breath, paused, and said, "You weary us with your questions; we will answer no more." She turned and hobbled out of sight into the darkness of the cave, the darkness that concealed her sister Ta and their humble living facilities.

The warrior stood respectfully motionless as the oracle withdrew, then turned east, toward where the last rays of sunlight lit the iced-in port of Ordunin and the cold sea beyond, and started thoughtfully down the hillside.

# CHAPTER ONE

The village of Skelleth was the northernmost limit of human civilization, a perpetually starving huddle of farmers and ice-cutters. It shrank with each succeeding ten-month winter. Its existence depended equally on the goats and hay of the farmers and on the declining trade in ice to cool the drinks of wealthy nobles to the south. This trade brought to the decaying community those many necessities they could not obtain from their own land, but was less each year as fewer of the ice-caravans survived the ravages of brigands and bankruptcy.

Although Skelleth was universally· acknowledged as the limit of human civilization, both humans and civilization could be found further north. The humans, however, were either the goat-herding nomads of the plains and foothills or the barbaric hunters and trappers of the snow-covered mountains, who were all too fond of banditry and murder and could hardly be called examples of civilization; the civilization was that of the overmen of the Northern Waste, driven there by the Racial Wars of three centuries before, and they were most assuredly not human.

It was because of these last that the Baron of Skelleth had seen fit to make the North Gate the only portion of the crumbling city wall to be guarded, although none of Skelleth's meager trade passed through the North Gate, even the wild trappers preferring to use the more accessible gates to east and west on their rare trading expeditions. At any hour, night or day, one of Skelleth's three dozen men-at-arms could be found huddled over a watch-fire in the shelter of the one remaining wall of the fallen gatehouse—assuming that the man assigned had not deserted his post. This cold and unrewarding duty made a convenient punishment for any guard who chanced to run afoul of the moody Baron's whims, and so was usually the lot of the younger and more cheerful among the company, as the Baron was prone to consider it a mortal offense should anyone be happy when he himself was sunk in one of his frequent and incapacitating fits of black depression.

Thus it was that Arner, youngest and most daring of the guard, was ordered to stand twenty-four hours of guard duty without relief at this unattractive spot; and it was scarcely surprising that the youth should abandon his post and be asleep in his sweetheart's arms when, for the first time in memory, someone did approach Skelleth down the ancient Wasteland Road.

Thus it was that Garth rode into Skelleth unannounced and unopposed, astride his great black warbeast, past the wide ring of abandoned, ruined homes and streets into the inhabited portion, his steel helmet glinting in the morning sunlight, his crimson cloak draped loosely across his shoulders. His gaze was fixed straight ahead, ignoring the ragged handful of villagers who first stared and then ran as he appeared in their midst.

Although Garth's noseless, leathery-brown face and glaring red eyes were enough to evoke horror among humans, it was quite possible that some of the villagers did not even notice him at first but ran from his mount, thinking it some unnatural monster of the Waste. It stood five feet high at the shoulder and measured eighteen feet from nose to tail, its sleek-furred feline form so superbly muscled that the weight of its armored rider was as nothing to it. Its wide, padded paws made no more sound than any lesser cat's and its slender tail curled behind it like a panther's. Like its master, the warbeast did not spare so much as a glance from its golden slit-eyes or a twitch of its stubby whiskers for the terror-stricken townspeople, but strode smoothly on, unaffected, with the superb grace of its catlike kind, triangular ears flattened against its head. Its normal walk was as fast as a man's trot, and the relentless onward flow of that great black body moving in utter silence through the icy mud of the streets was as terrifying in itself as the three-inch fangs that gleamed from its jaw.

As the screams and shouts of the fleeting villagers increased, a faint frown touched Garth's thin-lipped mouth, though his gaze never wavered; this noisy reception was not what he wanted. He slid back his cloak, revealing the steely gray breastplate and black mail beneath, and slid his double-edged battle-axe from its place on the saddle, carrying it loosely in his left hand. His right hand still held the guide-handle of the beast's halter, a guide that was more a formality than a necessity for a well-trained warbeast. Garth knew that his mount was the finest product of Kirpa's breeding farms, the end result of a thousand years of magically assisted crossbreeding and careful selection. Still, he kept the handle in hand, preferring to trust no creature save himself.

As Garth approached the market-square at the center of town, he found himself the object of a hundred curious stares. His lack of offensive action thus far had allowed the villagers to gather their nerve, and they now lined the street to watch him pass, their earlier shouting giving way to an awed silence; he was by far the most impressive sight Skelleth had seen in centuries. They gawked at the size of his mount, at his own seven-foot stature, at the gleaming axe in his hand, at the dull armor that protected him and, incidentally, hid the black fur that was one of the major differences between his race and humanity. He could not hide his lack of facial hair, his lack of a nose, nor the hollow cheeks and narrow lips which all combined to give his visage, to human eyes, much the appearance of a red-eyed skull.

Garth was not impressed with Skelleth. It certainly

failed to live up to the ancestral tales of a mighty
fortress standing eternally vigilant, barring his race
from the warm, lush south. Although the outer wall
had plainly once been a serious fortification, he had
seen several gaps in it as he approached, crumbled
sections wide enough for a dozen soldiers to walk
through abreast if they were willing to clamber over
loose stone. He could see why the wall went unre-
paired; the village guarded by this quondam barrier
was scarcely worth the trouble of taking that walk.
Quite aside from the foolishness of the crowd, even in
the parts not utterly ruinous, the half-timbered buildings that sagged with long years of harsh weather and
ill care were no better than the poorest sections of his
native Ordunin—rather worse, in truth, and the people, dirty, ragged, and flea-bitten, were worse still.
But then, they were merely humans.

There was a murmur among the villagers as half a
dozen men-at-arms belatedly appeared, their short
swords drawn. Garth looked at them in mild amusement, dropping his gaze at last, and halted his mount
with a soft word.

To the northerner, this pitiful sextet appeared as
harmless as as many geese; he had feared he would
be confronted by cavalry in plate armor, or at the
very least a few pikemen, not a handful of farmers in
rusty mail shirts carrying poorly forged swords half
the length of the broad blade that hung at his side.
Surely his ancestors had fought mightier foes than
these? It was clearly not just the wall that had decayed
over the years since the overmen had withdrawn into
the Northern Waste. Still, these were plainly the town
authorities or their representatives, and it was necessary to treat them diplomatically if he were to go on
about his business unhindered. It being the guest's
duty to speak before the host, he said, "Greetings, men
of Skelleth."

With some hesitation, the squad's captain—at least,
Garth assumed he was captain, since his helmet was

steel rather than leather—replied, "Greetings, over-man."

"I am Garth of Ordunin. I come in peace."

"Then why is your axe unsheathed?"

"I was unsure of my reception."

Hesitating once more, the captain said, "We have no quarrel with you."

Garth slid the axe back into its boot. "Then could you direct me to the King's Inn?"

The man gave directions, then paused, unsure of what to do next.

"May I pass?" Garth asked politely.

Well aware that, should the warbeast decide to pass, he and his men would have no chance of stopping it, the captain motioned his subordinates aside, and Garth continued on his way to the broken-down tavern that had been known for longer than anyone could recall as the King's Inn, despite the utter lack of any connection with any known monarch.

As the guard captain watched the looming figure of the overman recede, it struck him that he had not yet fulfilled his whole duty; two details remained. "Tarl, Thoromor, we must inform the Baron at once," he said. Ignoring the unhappy expressions of the two chosen to accompany him, he pointed to those not named and went on, "And you three will go see whether that monster killed Arner or whether the young fool deserted his post, and report back to me." The trio saluted and marched off as the captain cast a final glance at Garth's back, sparing himself a moment to envy the overman's armor and weapons before hurrying toward the Baron's mansion. The pair he took with him followed reluctantly, muttering over the unpleasant likelihood that their lord would be in one of his notorious fits of depression.

It was a sign of Skelleth's poverty that the Baron could afford neither palace nor castle, but made do with a house that was referred to as a mansion largely out of courtesy, facing the market-square and blocking a few winding streets that perforce ended in a short cross-alley along the rear of the Baron's home. Once these streets had been thoroughfares leading into the square when Skelleth had a less immediate government; but the first Baron had erected his domicile and seat of government with an utter disregard for anything except the appearance of its unbroken façade. Thus the alley that had once been an unimportant cross-street became even less important as the streets leading into it were cut off, and sank into a state of filth and disrepair unequaled anywhere in the kingdom of Eramma. It was on this alley that the King's Inn faced.

Garth's face, having no nose to wrinkle, showed no sign of disgust at his unhygienic surroundings as he led his mount into the stable beside the tavern, but he was disgusted nevertheless; no community of overmen, he told himself, would ever allow such feculence. Trying to ignore his environment, he made sure the warbeast was as comfortable as could be managed, removing the battle-axe from the saddle to prevent chafing where its haft slapped the creature's flank and cleaning the beast's catlike ears with the wire brush designed for that task. The creature accepted these attentions silently, as always. That done, the overman leaned the axe and his broadsword against one wall of the stall, as neither was suitable equipage for a visit to a tavern; his only weapon would be the foot-long dirk on his belt. Looking around, he spotted the stable-boy who had tremblingly refused to approach the monstrous beast, and strode over to him. The frightened youth cowered, but stood his ground.

"My warbeast will need feeding. See that he is brought meat, as much as you can carry, raw, and as fresh as possible. If he is not fed before I return, I will let him eat you instead. Is that clear?" The lad nodded, too frightened to speak. "Further, if any of my belongings are disturbed, I will hunt down and kill whoever is responsible. Here." He pulled a handful of gold from the pouch on his belt and dumped it in the boy's hands. The youth's eyes widened, his fear forgotten, though he remained unable to speak. Garth realized that he had probably just given away as much gold as the entire village possessed, but the thought did not bother him; he had plenty, and could expect good service if he were generous. Leaving the boy staring in disbelief at the wealth he held, the overman strode out of the stable toward the tavern.

Stepping inside the taproom door, Garth stopped for an instant in astonishment. Despite its ordure-coated, crumbling exterior, the King's Inn was as clean and orderly within as a well-kept ship. The floor was well-scrubbed oak, worn to a velvet smoothness by countless feet and shaped into hills and valleys that showed the tables had not been moved in generations; the walls were paneled in dark woods kept polished to a reflective gloss; the windows, though the glass was purple with age, were spotless and unbroken. The tables and chairs were solid, well-made pieces of the woodworker's art, worn, like the floor, to a beautiful softness. Most of one wall was taken up by a stone fireplace where a friendly blaze danced. Opposite it stood the barrels of beer and wine, their brass fittings polished and bright. The far wall was partially obscured by a staircase leading to an upper story, and various doors opened to either side.

Though it was too early in the day for even the lunchtime drinkers, half a dozen customers were sitting about; they had been talking cheerfully, but all conversation died when the overman entered. All eyes save two turned toward the armored monstrosity that stood in the doorway, blinking in surprise. The two that did not belonged to a figure that sat alone at a small table in the corner between the fireplace and the stairs, a figure bent with age whose only visible feature was a long white beard, the rest of his face and form being hidden by the tattered ruin of a hooded yellow cloak that he wore.

As Garth's moment of astonishment passed, he spotted this lone shape and wondered briefly why he did not look up as had his fellows. Perhaps he was deaf and had not noticed the silence, or blind, in which case he had no reason to raise his head. Both infirmities, Garth knew, were common among extremely aged humans. He returned his thoughts to his quest and realized that this ancient was the only one present fitting the oracle's description. Although the other customers, apparently all farmers, were far from well-dressed, none were in rags. Only the old man wore yellow, the others being variously clad in gray, brown, and a paler gray that must once have been white. With a mental shrug, though outwardly impassive, Garth crossed the room to the shadowed corner where the old man sat, and seated himself at the other side of the table.

The old man gave no sign that he was aware of the newcomer.

The other customers, after following the overman across the room with their eyes, now turned back to their own conversations. Garth was unsure whether his sensitive ears had caught the phrase "Should have known" being muttered at another table.

After a moment, when the old man remained utterly motionless, Garth hesitantly broke the silence by saying, in a low voice, "I seek one called the Forgotten King."

"Who are you?" The voice was little more than a whisper, as dry as autumn leaves, horribly dry and harsh, yet clear and steady.

"I am called Garth, of Ordunin."

"Your title?"

"What?" Garth was taken aback.

"What title do you bear?"

"Tell me first of him whom I seek."

"I am he; answer me your title."

Reluctantly, the overman answered, "I am Prince of Ordunin, and Lord of the Overmen of the Northern Waste."

At last the old man moved, raising his head to gaze at Garth. The overman saw that his face was as dry and wrinkled as a mummy's, and his eyes so deeply sunken that they remained invisible in the shadow of the dark yellow hood. Garth had a momentary uncomfortable impression that there were no eyes, that he was looking at empty sockets, but he dismissed it as a trick of the light.

"What would you have of me?"

"I have been told, O King, that you can grant me a boon I desire."

"Who has told you this?"

"An oracle."

"What oracle?"

"One among my own people. You would not have heard of her."

"She must have heard of me."

Unwillingly, unsettled by those darkened eyes, Garth replied, "She and her sister are called the Wise Women of Ordunin."

There was no reply.

"They have said that you alone may grant what I ask."

"Ah. What do you ask?"

"I am weary of life as it is, in which decay and death are everywhere. I am tired of being insignificant in the cosmos."

"Such is the lot of all, be they man or overman." The dry monotone was unchanged, but Garth thought a glint of light touched the hidden eyes. He was comforted by this proof that there were indeed eyes there.

"I would not have it so. O King, I know my place in the cosmos, I know I cannot change the stars nor alter the fate of the world, although I would like to; that is not what I ask. If I cannot change the world, then I would influence the dwellers therein. I would have it that my name shall be known so long as any living thing shall move upon the earth or sea, that I shall be famed throughout the world."

The figure in yellow stirred. "Why would you have this?"

"Vanity, O King."

"You know it for vanity? There is no other purpose?"

"There is no other purpose possible to such a desire."

"Think you not that your desire exceeds reason, even in vanity? What will it profit you that you be remembered when dead?"

"Nothing. But I would know while I yet live that I shall be thus remembered, for this knowledge will comfort me when it comes my turn to die."

"So be it, then, Garth of Ordunin; what you wish shall be yours if you serve me without fail in certain tasks. I, too, have an unfulfilled desire, the realization of which requires certain magic I do not now possess, and I swear by my heart and all the gods that if I achieve my goal with your aid, then your name shall be known as long as there is life upon this earth."

The old man's face had slipped back into shadow as he made this speech, but Garth thought he detected a smile as he said, "I shall serve you, O King."

"We shall see. I must first set you a trial of sorts, for I dare not send an incompetent about certain businesses. I must also be sure I will not be bothered unnecessarily."

Garth made no reply as the hooded face sank back to its original contemplative position, so that only the thin white beard showed. It was some ten minutes before the dry voice spoke again.

"You will bring me the first living thing you find in the ancient crypts beneath Mormoreth."

"Mormoreth?"

"A city, far to the east. But details can wait. Fetch me food and drink." The ancient head rose once more, and although the eyes were as invisible as ever, the wrinkled lips were twisted upward in a hideous grin.

# CHAPTER TWO

It was almost two days later when the overman remounted his warbeast and rode toward the East Gate. Much of the intervening time had been spent deciding what he might need and making sure he had it. Although he had come from Ordunin equipped for most eventualities, he had not prepared for bringing a live captive of some sort back across plains and mountains. He had no idea what the first living thing he would encounter in the crypts would be, and had to consider every possibility from insect to elephant. He could only hope that it was not a dragon he was being sent after, although even that possibility was provided for as best he could manage with an asbestos blanket and several heavy chains. His first inclination had been to acquire cages of various sizes, but he quickly realized that that was impractical and settled on a single cage big enough for a large cat or small dog, but with a wire mesh so fine it would hold most insects or spiders. Should his quarry prove to be larger, he had several ropes and chains of various weights, and a short bolt of gray cloth which could be used for binding or muzzling. He had determined to make do with his usual three weapons, axe, sword, and dagger, rather than weigh himself and his mount down any further with more specialized gear; as with restraints, he could only hope he was not being sent after a dragon.

Besides these special preparations, he of course made the usual ones, checking and refilling his canteen and water-cask, obtaining food that would not spoil, and making certain that both he and his beast were as well fed and healthy as he could contrive.

The Forgotten King watched all these preparations in silent amusement, refusing to offer any advice or assistance other than a repetition of the original charge and directions for reaching Mormoreth, which were absurdly simple inasmuch as an old highway ran almost directly thither from Skelleth's East Gate, requiring only that a traveler know which fork to take at each of three turnings. He also consumed, at Garth's expense, an amount of food and wine astonishing for one so old and thin. But prices being what they were in Skelleth, this did little to deplete the overman's supply of gold.

While these preparations were being made, there was some stir in the village over a local event that did not strike Garth as being in any way relevant to himself; a man named Arner had been sentenced to decapitation by the Baron, who was said to be in an even fouler temper than was customary in the spring and to be behaving most erratically. When Garth overheard this, whispered by villagers torn between excitement at the prospect of a public execution and anger at the harshness of the decision, he shrugged it off as yet another manifestation of the difference between the cultures of Skelleth and Ordunin, an event that could only happen among humans. Unfamiliar as he was with human emotions, he did not notice the resentful glances invariably cast in his direction when the subject came up. He remained calmly unconcerned about the entire matter, riding through the village streets and out the gate unaware of the hate-filled glances he received, most especially from the Baron's guards, the companions of the doomed man. The hatred of his own kind was never visible in face or manner, but only in words and actions, so that he was utterly incapable of seeing the human emotion for what it was. Nor would he have cared if he did recognize it, for he thought little better of men than he did of dogs.

His journey was uneventful at first, a peaceful ride down a well-used highway where the snow had been pounded flat and hard by the feet of farmers and caravans and was only beginning to show signs of melting into the muddy slush it would soon become. But with his turning at the first fork, the way became much worse, as no trade passed along the road to Mormoreth and he was beyond all but the furthest farms. The road here was buried in largely untrodden snow, its presence discernible only because of the relatively large spaces between the struggling trees, the greater-than-elsewhere number of tracks, both human and animal —the human, as often as not, made by bare feet; the locals must be either very poor or very barbaric, Garth thought—and the irregularly spaced milestones, which were often buried, only a mound or small drift in the even snow cover indicating their presence.

The snow actually did little to slow the warbeast, whose padded paws and long legs had been intended for all weather, but the difficulty of being sure of the road's location caused Garth to keep the beast's speed down and to stop every so often to reconnoiter. As a result, it was a full week before he crossed the hills onto the Plain of Derbarok, a distance he could ordinarily have traveled in half that time. That week included two brief delays to allow his warbeast to hunt its own food. Even had he wanted to, it would have been impossible for Garth to carry with him enough meat to feed the immense hybrid, especially in view of its preference for fresh meat. Instead he loosed the beast every third evening after he had made camp. Ordinarily it would have been back by morning, but the poor hunting the region allowed had kept it away until almost noon on both occasions so far. Entering the open plain worried the overman slightly, as he knew nothing of what wildlife was to be found in such terrain. Although the beast was usually superbly obedient, if it became hungry enough it would run amok, willing to devour even its master, and Garth had no misconceptions as to how dangerous the creature could be. Even with axe and broadsword, he had grave doubts that he could handle a starving warbeast.

It was with great relief, therefore, that he caught sight of large animals grazing in the distance. They disappeared over the horizon before he could decide whether to loose his mount or not, but he knew that where there was any wildlife at all his beast would be able to find sufficient prey. This weight lifted from his mind, he rode on calmly, meditating on his appointed task, wondering what manner of living thing he would find and running through every contingency he could think of, to be certain he was equipped as well as he could manage. The matter of feeding the warbeast was ignored, as it had been only two days since its last meal, the normal interval between feedings being seventy-two hours.

Having decided that he was indeed sufficiently well prepared, Garth pondered the purpose of his mission. The most likely products of his quest would be serpents, rats, or spiders, and he could see no point in the capture of vermin. The Forgotten King meant this errand as a trial, so there would be difficulties encountered. It would appear that his intended quarry was not mere vermin, then. But how could the old man be sure that the quarry he wanted would be the first living thing that Garth found? It seemed unlikely in the extreme that he had been to Mormoreth himself recently . . .

His thoughts were interrupted by a low growl from his mount. Its catlike ears were laid back, as if in preparation for battle. Clearly, something had disturbed the great black beast. He looked at it questioningly, but it gave no indication of the direction from which danger threatened. Instead it stopped dead in its tracks, its nostrils flared, its head lowered as if ready either to receive a charge or to launch one itself; yet the head wavered slightly from side to side. The beast was plainly as unsure in which quarter the threat lay as was its master, and Garth thought it was unusually uneasy.

He unsheathed his broadsword and held it at ready; his own senses had as yet detected no sign of danger, but he trusted the keener perceptions of his mount. It had saved him before.

His eyes swept the plain, a vast expanse of drying mud, the winter snow melted on this side of the hills. It seemed empty as far as the horizon ahead and to either side, while behind lay only the barren, unthreatening ridge. He could see no danger. Closer at hand he saw no snakes, no pitfalls that could account for the warbeast's actions. Thoroughly unsettled, he sat unmoving upon his unmoving mount for perhaps a minute. When no threat manifested itself, he cautiously urged the animal forward, his sword still in his hand.

The beast took a single step, then froze again. Garth did not need to wonder why. He himself sat utterly motionless for a few brief seconds that seemed like long, slow minutes as he struggled to accept the evidence of his senses.

He was staring into the face of a fur-clad human, not fifteen feet away.

The face had not approached, not slid in from the side, not swooped down from above, not risen out of the ground; it had simply appeared!

Attached to the face was a lean body wrapped in gray furs and seated upon a beast thoroughly unlike Garth's own, a brown beast with a long, narrow muzzle, great round eyes on either side of its head of a brown a shade darker than its hide, a shock of long black hair starting between its ears and running down the back of its neck.

Garth took this in instantly, without any conscious reaction; indeed, the image of that bizarre creature and its barbaric rider burned itself into his mind to the momentary exclusion of all else.

The rider had skin burnt brown by the sun and wind, but still paler than the overman's own. He had dirty, ragged black hair trailing to his shoulders; his features were contorted into an expression that conveyed nothing to his inhuman observer; and his right arm was raised above his head, clutching a long, curved, dull-gray sword, which was sweeping down and to the side, a motion that, when combined with the forward charge of his mount, would bring the blade sweeping into the eyes of Garth's warbeast.

This all flashed before the overman in seeming slow motion as he sat frozen in astonishment. Then time started to resume its normal pace as he brought his own blade up to meet and parry the attack.

It was only after he heard the clash of steel on steel, heard the warbeast roar in anger, felt it moving under him as it swung its head aside, and felt himself slipping from the saddle that he realized the attacker was not alone; at least a dozen of the strange animals and their barbaric riders were approaching from a dozen directions.

The combination of utter unbelieving astonishment, the sudden thrashing of his mount, and his own sideways lunge in parrying the first attack did what it would ordinarily take several men to do; Garth lost his balance. Rather than fight to regain it, which would waste precious seconds, he swung his legs free and slid to the ground, standing beside his beast. This action also served to guard his rear, as the furry bulk of the animal was almost as impenetrable as a stone wall at his back.

Fortunately for the overman, his opponents were disorganized, attacking without any order or plan. When he hit the ground he found the one facing him all but motionless, while the others remained out of reach. Never one to miss an opportunity, he drove his sword forward with all the power he could manage at the extreme reach necessary to hit a mounted warrior; it was sufficient. The point of the blade ripped through the man's fur jacket, through the rusty mail underneath, and into his chest. He let out a gasping moan, and his eyes sprang wide. Garth guessed he had pierced a lung. His face grim, the overman withdrew his blade, unleashing a gout of blood from both the wound and the man's gaping mouth. The bar-

barian fell forward and to the left, tumbling messily
from his mount, which shied away in terror, eyes rolling.

Even as the man died, Garth heard two screams,
one human and one hideously inhuman; the warbeast
was defending itself. Its low growl could be heard as
the screaming subsided, but Garth dared not take
the time to look to see what was happening; he was
again beset, this time by a yelling maniac charging at
him with saber swinging. Not caring to risk the
strength of his sword's metal against the swooping arc
of the saber, Garth ducked low and thrust his blade
at the man's mount. The saber whistled over his head.
His own weapon slashed open the animal's belly and
was almost torn from his grasp by the momentum of
the creature's charge. The thing screamed, horribly,
then fell, flinging its master aside; Garth could spare
no further attention for it as two more mounted warriors approached, much more cautiously.

This pair showed the first teamwork the attackers
had displayed; approaching from opposite sides,
they swung their blades in unison, both aiming for the
body rather than the head. The overman parried one
blade while attempting to dodge the other, but was
not totally successful. His breastplate took the blow
he had attempted to dodge, the sword scraping across
it, bruising his body beneath, while his parry locked
with the other blade, notching the overman's weapon
and requiring three vital seconds to untangle.

Thus delayed, Garth was unable to defend himself
against a second blow from his other antagonist. Seeing the blade approaching, he attempted to dodge
again. He was lucky; the blade became entangled in
his cloak, grazing his shoulder lightly. Awkwardly,
Garth dropped his left hand from his sword hilt and
drew his dagger. Maintaining his guard as best he
could with the broadsword on his right, he turned his
attention to the left and hacked with his dagger at
the hand that held the entangled sword. The man

released his weapon, his wrist gouged messily, and Garth turned his attention once again to the right.

Throughout this exchange Garth could feel the warbeast moving about behind him, and a constant accompaniment of growling, screaming, and shouting filled the overman's ears. Rage began to overcome him, and rather than continue the defensive, cautious fighting he had been using up to that point, he went on the offensive. Depending on his vastly superior strength and reach, he drove forward, blade swinging.

From that point on, things happened too fast for Garth to follow consciously: he hacked down at least two more warriors, one mounted and one on foot; at least one sword broke before the fury of his onslaught; blood spattered his cloak and armor, some of it his own, but mostly human.

Then, abruptly, the fight was over. A cry went up calling the retreat, and Garth found himself standing alone, ten feet from his mount, with dead and dying men strewn about him. His rage subsided abruptly, to be replaced with revulsion; he did not approve of unnecessary bloodshed, and this gory mess seemed definitely unnecessary.

Disgusted, he looked about, ignoring the handful of survivors fleeing to the southeast. Nine men lay unmoving around him, with three of their strange beasts. Three of the men were obviously dead, their throats ripped out by the warbeast. Two of the animals were the same. The third downed animal was the one Garth had gutted with his sword. The overman was not certain whether a trace of life remained or not. Since he obviously could do nothing for the creature if it still lived, he killed it as swiftly as he could with his sword.

Of the six men still more or less intact, investigation showed three dead of sword wounds, one with a broken neck resulting from being flung from his mount, one with a slashed wrist and a gash across his chest, unconscious from loss of blood, and the last, his leg trapped beneath his fallen mount, still alive and struggling.

His struggles grew frantic as Garth approached, then ceased when he realized that he could not free himself. The overman looked at him and, seeing no obvious wounds, decided the man could wait. Ignoring the barbarian's terrified cringing, he motioned for the warbeast to stand guard over the trapped man. The creature padded silently over and stood motionless, its fearsome, blood-soaked jaws directly above the man's face, dripping gore on the mud by his ear.

Garth then turned his attention to the unconscious warrior; stripping off the man's armor and clothing, he used the cloth linings to improvise bandages and bind the wounds. He was displeased to see the dull white fabric turn bright red in a matter of seconds; the cuts were deeper than they appeared. Momentarily leaving the man where he lay, he fetched his own medical supplies from the pack on his mount's back.

The trapped barbarian asked hesitantly, "What are you doing?"

Garth did not bother to answer, but returned to his patient and carefully removed the bloody bandages. He cleaned the wounds as best he could, applied what healing herbs and drugs he felt he could spare, and bound them anew with fresh wrappings. When he was satisfied that he had done all he could, he arranged the warrior as comfortably as he could on the man's own furs, covered him with furs from one of his dead companions, and placed a sword beside the man's right hand so that he could defend himself against any carrion-eaters that might wake him.

This done, he turned his attention to his own wounds; none were serious, but there were many of them. He had undoubtedly lost at least as much blood as the unconscious human he had just treated. Upon realizing this, he realized as well that he was very weary and that his entire body was laced with pain. Still, he drove himself to complete the dressing of his injuries and then to turn at last to his conscious captive.

Standing beside the warbeast, looking down at the pinned barbarian, Garth demanded, "Are you in pain?"

"My leg hurts."

"The trapped one?"

"Yes."

The overman muttered a command to the warbeast. It growled softly, then reached down, grabbed the dead animal's ruined neck in its teeth, and lifted the creature's front half off the ground as if it weighed no more than a mouthful of hay. The barbarian quickly pulled his leg free, and the warbeast bit down, so that the animal's body fell heavily to one side while its head fell to the other. Garth watched as a curious grimace crossed the face of his captive. He had had too little contact with humanity to realize that the man was struggling to keep from vomiting. The barbarian turned his head away from the grisly ruin of his mount and the unsettling sight of the warbeast chewing contentedly, and asked his captor, "What are you going to do with me?"

"Does your leg still hurt?"

"Yes." The man made a half-hearted attempt to get to his feet and failed. The overman stooped, and felt the damaged leg.

"It's broken; lie still."

It took the overman some time to locate a usable splint, but eventually he broke the haft from an axe he found among the scattered debris of the battle and bound it in place with leather from the reins of the man's mount. As he checked the bindings, the man said, "I am Elmil of Derbarok."

"I am Garth of Ordunin."

"What are you going to do with me?"

"I have not decided."

"What about—"

"Wait." Garth did not want to answer questions; he had not yet finished his self-imposed task of cleaning up after the battle. Ignoring Elmil temporarily, he systematically stripped the seven dead warriors, leaving them lying naked in the icy mud, then sorted through their belongings, and added those items he thought might prove useful or valuable to his own pack. The remainder he dumped in a heap beside the unconscious man he had earlier bandaged. Elmil watched these actions in confused silence, then demanded, "Why do you leave them naked?"

"As easier prey for carrion-eaters, so that your living companion will have more time to recover."

Elmil made no answer.

"Are the men of Derbarok honorable?" Garth inquired.

Elmil was astonished. "We are bandits and thieves who use magic trickery. How can you even ask?"

"It is said there is honor amongst thieves. I want to know whether I may take your word of honor rather than tying you up while I sleep."

"My word of honor?"

"Your word of honor that you will not escape, nor harm me nor my warbeast."

"But you have no way of knowing whether my word is good or not, save my word."

"This is true. But if you break it, you will die. If you escape, I will hunt you down. If you harm me, my warbeast will hunt you down."

"Then why do you ask?"

"I would have your word so that you will not feel compelled to attempt escape despite the consequences."

"I don't understand."

"It is not necessary that you understand, merely that you either give your word of honor that you will neither escape nor attempt to harm me, or permit me to bind you." The overman's faint tone of annoyance failed to register with the barbarian, but he had exhausted his objections.

"I could not escape with a broken leg in any case; I will give you my word."

"Very good. Then we will rest." It was scarcely sunset, but the overman's loss of blood had tired him. As he was preparing to bed down, himself on his bedroll and Elmil a few feet away on furs that had once belonged to his fellow bandits, the warbeast growled hungrily. Garth called to it, and it began contentedly eating what remained of Elmil's dead mount.

The action reminded Garth of a question. "What do you call those animals?"

"Do you mean the horses?"

"Horses?" Garth had heard the word before; to the inhabitants of the Northern Waste, horses were a vague legend. They were not suited to the climate and had long since died out in the northern lands, but they apparently still throve further south.

Elmil paused, then asked a question of his own. "What is your beast's name?"

"Name?"

"What do you call him?"

"Nothing. It is my beast. It needs no name of its own."

Elmil paused again, musing, then said, "I will call him Koros, for the Arkhein god of war."

Garth remarked absently, "It is a neuter, not a male." He considered briefly, then said, "It is a good name. Hear you, beast? Your name is Koros." The beast growled in answer as Garth rolled over and went to sleep.

# CHAPTER THREE

Garth awoke at the first light of dawn, and was gratified to see Elmil still asleep nearby. Had the man fled during the night, Garth's quest to Mormoreth might have been delayed for as much as a week in tracking him down and killing him.

Although it was not yet light enough to travel, the overman began packing and loading. There was not much to be done, and he finished in less than ten minutes. The sound was enough to waken Elmil, however, and the bandit lent what aid he could in tying the furs he had slept in over the immense pack on the warbeast's back. As he did, Garth noticed him glancing frequently at the creature's monstrous head and at the scanty remains of his horse. When the loading was complete, Garth said, "You never saw a warbeast before."

"No."

"Nor an overman?"

"No; I had heard tales of overmen, but never have I heard of such a beast."

"They are bred by my people in the valley of Kirpa. The first were an admixture of panther, dog, and ass used in the Racial Wars three hundreds years ago."

Elmil studied the beast. It was plainly descended from some great cat, and its disproportionately long legs could be from its donkey ancestry, but he could see no trace of the canine. Its huge, sleek black body bore not the slightest resemblance to the scruffy wild dogs he was familiar with. But then, overmen were said to be derived from humanity, and the seven-foot horror he had fought the previous day had not seemed in any way human.

His thoughts were interrupted by the overman's voice. "How did your band appear so abruptly yesterday?"

"By magic; we approached you while invisible."

"How was this magic worked?"

"Khand, our chieftain, had a talisman called the Jewel of Blindness. I do not know how it worked, save that it turned us all invisible, inaudible, and intangible when we touched it."

"Where did your chieftain get this? It would take a mighty wizard to make such a thing, and such a wizard would not be leading bandits."

"He got it from Shang."

"Who is Shang?"

"Have you never heard of him?" Elmil was plainly surprised.

"You had not heard of warbeasts," Garth reminded him.

"He is the mightiest wizard in Orûn. He came from the far south, and took Mormoreth for his own. All Orûn fears him."

"Why did he give Khand this talisman?"

"We had a bargain with him; in exchange for the talisman, we were to stay out of the valley Mormoreth lies in, and slay any who tried to approach it."

"Khand still has the talisman, then."

"What?" Again, Elmil's surprise was obvious. "Khand lies dead, where you slew him."

Garth looked where the bandit pointed; the corpse indicated was one of the men Koros had killed. Without further comment, the overman strode to where the unconscious barbarian he had bandaged the preceding day lay, and retrieved one of the furs he had been wrapped in; in doing so, Garth noticed that the man had died during the night.

The fur he had recovered was a bloodstained vest, which the overman remembered as coming from Khand's body. A quick investigation located a concealed inner pocket, which held a hard object perhaps the size of a walnut. Being careful not to touch the object. Garth opened the pocket and peered inside. It contained a pure-white gem that glittered in the dim morning light. Without comment, he carefully dumped the jewel into his own cloak pocket, still without touching it, and tossed the vest aside. Then, turning back to where Elmil stood dwarfed by the warbeast, he announced, "We go."

"Where?"

"To Mormoreth." He grinned as Elmil started to protest. "I intend to give Shang back his trinket."

The bandit thought better of further objections and permitted the overman to lift him, broken leg dragging awkwardly, onto Koros' broad back, like a child being placed astride a pony. Garth himself remained afoot, not wishing to overload the beast, and thus they set out along the muddy path that was euphemistically called a road.

Perhaps a quarter of an hour passed before either spoke; then Garth inquired, "Does Shang live in the crypts?"

Startled, Elmil asked, "What crypts?"

"You said that Shang dwells in Mormoreth. Does he live in the crypts beneath the city?"

"Shang lives in the palace. I know of no crypts."

This answer both relieved and troubled Garth. He was relieved in that he had not considered the possibility of being required to capture a powerful wizard, and was glad that he apparently wouldn't have to; but he was worried by Elmil's ignorance of the crypts. It occurred to him that he might well have to search the entire city to locate an entrance, a prospect that did not appeal to him in view of Shang's presence there.

They continued in silence, and the day passed without incident. They made good time, considering the fact that Garth was on foot, as here on the open plain there was no mistaking the road. Further, Elmil was thoroughly familiar with the terrain, having spent most of his life riding across it with his fellow bandits.

Shortly before sunset, Garth noticed that several sets of hoofprints had converged on the road, bound in the same direction that he and his captive were taking. His suspicions were corroborated when Elmil remarked, "These are left by my comrades; I recognize the bent horseshoe mark that Dansin's mount Eknissa makes."

Garth made no reply for several minutes. Then he asked, "Does this road lead to your home?"

"No; our village is well to the south, along the old highway to Kholis. This road leads only to the Annamar Pass."

"Then why would your band take it?"

Elmil looked troubled, though Garth did not recognize what the change in expression signified. He replied, "I don't know. The Pass leads down through the hills into Orûn, through the valley of Mormoreth, and we have sworn not to trespass there. Perhaps they will turn aside, seeking a cache of supplies such as we have secreted along all the roads."

"Do you know of such a cache between here and this pass you have mentioned?"

The bandit's worried look deepened. "No."

The overman made no further comment. In renewed silence the trio of man, beast, and overman continued into the gathering darkness.

They made camp late that night and arose early, getting underway once more while dawn was still a pale glimmer in the east. Elmil wondered as to the reason for this, but decided against asking. He had begun to realize that Garth was reluctant to speak with him, though he had no idea why this was the case. He put it down to his status as a captive.

Garth, meanwhile, was wondering whether it was really worth keeping this foul little thief around. He could make much better time without him; also, the human had a rather unpleasant odor, and his appearance was hardly endearing. The overman wondered what use a nose was, and how men saw through such pale little eyes. He had never had much contact with humans, and was not particularly enjoying it. His brief stay in Skelleth had given him a very low opinion of humanity, and this barbarian had done little to raise it. However, he had wounded the man and separated him from his people, which obligated him to look after his welfare, at least until the broken leg was healed; and the man could provide much useful information about the area, as well as being a possible hostage should his tribesmen attack again. This last item seemed important, since it appeared that the bandits did indeed intend to ambush him, probably in the Annamar Pass. Why else would they take this road? He considered altering his route to avoid such a possible ambush, but decided against it; he had no desire to get himself lost in strange country, and doubted that Elmil would be much use as a guide once they were off the plain. Another possibility was to attempt to use the talisman he had taken from Khand's corpse, which Elmil called the Jewel of Blindness; but that held little appeal. Garth distrusted all magic, as he distrusted anything he didn't understand, and did not care to risk the possible consequences of misusing such a powerful charm without a much better reason than the possibility of an ambush by a small band of vengeance-bent bandits that he had already defeated once.

In the end, he decided simply to proceed as he had planned, keeping a wary eye out for any possible ambuscade or sharp-shooting archers. The latter seemed unlikely, as he had seen no bows nor other long-range weaponry in the bandits' possession, nor found so much as a simple sling on the corpses he had stripped; but it never hurt to consider all possibilities.

For example, it had not escaped him that the bandits might have gone seeking reinforcements, perhaps even the aid of this mysterious wizard, Shang. It seemed of rather low probability, given the abject fear of the magician displayed by Elmil, and even less likely that Shang would give aid if asked, but the eventuality should be considered. Thus, Garth considered it, and concluded that he was simply too ignorant of the ways of wizards to devise an appropriate course of action. There were no wizards among the overmen of Ordunin, nor had he met any human wizards, unless the Forgotten King was such. He had seen minor exhibitions of so-called magic which appeared to be little more than sleight-of-hand, but he could not totally discount all tales of sorcerous doings as such simple trickery. In fact, he had once seen a roaring thunderstorm appear from a clear sky, supposedly the work of three wizards working in concert, to aid a pirate raid on Ordunin. The raid had failed, and three of the five pirate vessels had been sunk; the storm had had no significant effect on the battle. It was also said that the breeding farms at Kirpa used magic to make possible hybrids that nature would not permit, such as his own warbeast. In fact, according to legend, the entire race of overmen was the result of a wizard's experiment some thousand years earlier. Garth was unsure how valid this latter rumor was.

In short, without a doubt his most direct contact with magic to date, and the most powerful magic he had ever received reliable word of, was the invisibility charm used by the bandits in their initial assault. That now lay safely in the pocket of his cloak. However, in all likelihood that was not Shang's most powerful device; if it were, he would hardly have entrusted it to a barbaric group of thieves.

Therefore, Garth concluded, he did not want to combat this enchanter. Truthfully, he did not even want to meet him, let alone risk antagonizing him; but it seemed inevitable that they would have some sort of contact.

The problem, therefore, was to keep all contact with Shang as amicable as possible. And that was not something that could be prepared in advance, but must be dealt with when the moment arrived. Thus he put aside consideration of the matter, consoling himself with a reminder that in all likelihood the bandits had no intention of seeking Shang's help after all.

So it was that Garth spent the remaining three days of the journey across the Plain of Derbarok alternately running through the same arguments mentally and relaxedly watching the rather drab scenery slowly inch by. The road became progressively muddier. Some stretches were so lost in the mire that Garth mounted the warbeast behind Elmil until they were past, rather than struggle through on foot with his boots filling with the knee-deep and still cold muck. The animal, which Elmil insisted on calling Koros at every opportunity, did not seem to object. Its own huge padded paws moved as smoothly and gracefully through these morasses as the oars of a well-run galley through the sea, and its pace remained constant regardless of load or terrain, save only when it slowed to accommodate Garth's less rapid pace. The overman began to appreciate how wise he had been to accept the creature in lieu of further tribute from the colony of overmen at Kirpa. It was clearly worth more than the token annual payment of grain it had replaced, even considering Ordunin's perpetual near-starvation. Prior to embarking on this quest Garth had rarely ridden it, since he had done little casual traveling and had fought no wars save by sea, against the depredations and occasional raids of the pirates of the Sea of Mori; he had had no opportunity to observe just how indomitable the beast was. There was, indeed, something more than mortal about its serene confidence in its own power, and he had to admit that naming it for a war-god seemed fitting.

When the overman sent the warbeast off to hunt its twice-weekly meal on the third night following the battle, it returned shortly after midnight, well fed, as it had not been in the forests west of Derbarok. Garth was pleased by this, as he was rather fond of the monster as well as impressed by it. Elmil, however, reacted with revulsion the following morning when he woke to find the only physical evidence of the hunt a pool of drying blood that had dripped from the animal's jaws during the night. Despite the bandit's admiration of Koros' power and grace, the beast both frightened and horrified him.

It was on the fourth day, shortly before sunset, with the eastern hills—which were actually good-sized mountains, in Garth's opinion—looming before them, and Garth riding and musing on his mount's virtues, that Elmil let out a sudden cry.

"Look! On the hilltop!"

Garth turned his gaze to follow the man's pointing finger, but saw nothing. He looked at him questioningly.

"I thought I saw a man."

"Was he of your band?"

"I think he may have been. I'm not sure."

With a wordless noise, Garth sat back in the saddle, scanning the horizon and ignoring Elmil's worried expression as the bandit twisted around to look at him. Seeing nothing, he glanced at the ground; seeing that they were past the pool of mud that had driven him to mount, he swung himself off Koros' back to resume his weary walking. Elmil continued to watch him worriedly for several minutes, but said nothing, and finally turned his attention back to the approaching mountains.

To Garth, the sighting plainly indicated that he was indeed walking into an ambush in the Annamar Pass; but, having already decided his course of action, he merely continued on as before. His only concession was to stand watch half that night while Elmil slept, then sleep whilst Elmil watched. Garth would have waited up much of the night in any case, as once again he let Koros hunt, rather than risk being unable to find game in the mountains. By referring to it as "standing guard," he allayed much of Elmil's growing uneasiness. He used Koros' return, shortly after midnight, as the signal to change the watch, and was mildly amused to see, as he dropped off to sleep. Elmil watching in horror as the warbeast licked blood from its curving front claws, claws that glittered red and bone-white in the moonlight.

It was still an hour before dawn when Garth awoke again, his light slumber broken by Elmil's first snore; despite his fears, the bandit had dozed off. No harm was done, though; rather, it merely meant the day would have an early start. After burying the ashes of their campfire and repacking their supplies, the overman woke his captive just long enough to get him perched firmly astride the warbeast, and set out toward the hills as the barbarian fell asleep again, bobbing gently in the saddle.

By the time Elmil woke fully, the sun was visible above the mountains and the road was slanting upward enough to make walking difficult. By noon the party was well into the mountains, and the road was again level. This was the Annamar Pass, several hundred feet above the level of the plain, but thousands of feet below the peaks on either side.

It was here that Garth fully expected an ambush to occur, and his wary alertness gradually changed to a growing apprehension as no attack came. Why were the bandits so slow to make their move? Was there, perhaps, something up here that had slain them and now lay lurking somewhere, ready to kill him as well? Or were they merely biding their time, to relax his vigilance?

Elmil, in the meantime, seemed utterly unworried. He had little to fear from any possible ambush, since the ambushers were his own tribesmen; although he felt no particular need of rescue from his inhuman captor, he had no objection to such an event. Garth had not mentioned the possibility of an ambush to him, but Elmil was not so blind as to miss the significance of sighting one of his comrades apparently standing lookout the preceding day. In fact, since it provided an acceptable explanation of why the bandits had taken this route, it relieved much of his earlier uneasiness. Thus he was highly amused by Garth's reaction when some small animal cracked a nut somewhere behind them. Far more nervous than he would ever have willingly admitted, the overman whirled at the sharp sound and stood with drawn sword at ready, glaring back down the road. Relaxing slowly, he turned forward once more and carefully sheathed his blade to find Elmil attempting to smother a grin and Koros waiting impatiently. Embarrassed, he said nothing, but merely marched on.

When sunset arrived they were perhaps two thirds of the way through the pass, and the road had begun to slope downward. Garth had finally decided that there would be no ambush and relaxed somewhat, though he was still worried by the mystery of why the bandits had taken this road. He considered discussing the matter with Elmil, but decided against it.

Elmil, meanwhile, had decided that his tribesmen were planning a midnight assault, the standard method for dealing with well-armed caravans; he debated mentioning this to the overman, but decided against it. Despite Garth's mercy in letting him live and even bandaging his leg, he was still at least nominally an enemy. Besides, the idea was so obvious that he was sure the overman had already thought of it.

That Garth had not in fact thought of it was a sign of his inexperience; in the past his only battles had been by sea, against pirates unfamiliar with Ordunin's waters, who dared not move at night for fear of ramming one another or running aground on reefs and rocks. He had not yet adjusted his thinking to allow for a new enemy, despite his presence in a new land. In truth, he had done very little real thinking of any sort since his decision to seek out the Wise Women of Ordunin, but had been allowing himself to be swept along by his determination to fulfill his quest for immortal fame.

Thus, when they made camp, Elmil carefully arranged his sleeping-furs well away from the fire, and well away from both overman and warbeast, so as to avoid being accidentally caught up in the melee. Garth noticed this, but guessed it to be merely a result of Elmil's distrust of Koros and failed to see its true significance. He had no objection, especially since it put the bandit further downwind. He sat up for a few hours but decided that a proper watch was unnecessary, particularly in view of how little sleep he had managed the preceding night, and went to sleep shortly before midnight.

It was three hours later that he was awakened by a growl from his beast. He was instantly alert, reaching for his battle-axe, which lay in its accustomed place close by his side. As his eyes adjusted to the darkness he saw three men on horseback, armed with lances, standing on the road perhaps fifty feet away.

Koros was awake and wary, standing over the supplies and growling; Elmil was still asleep, and a fourth rider had dismounted to stand over him with a spear at his throat.

"I'll watch this traitor. You three kill the animal, and then we'll handle the overman." It was the man on foot who spoke.

Not wishing to lose either mount or captive, Garth leapt to his feet, axe in hand, and charged toward the intruders. To his astonishment, he was stopped short perhaps two yards from his bed, rebounding as if from an unseen wall. One of the horsemen laughed nastily, and all grinned as Garth groped his way along the barrier, to find that it extended in a full circle some six or seven yards in diameter, bringing him back to where he began, facing the bandits. It extended to the ground throughout, regardless of the irregular terrain, and higher in the center than he could reach, when he leapt with one arm extended upward his hand met no resistance. When he tried to pull himself up the invisible wall, he could get no grip. It was as if the barrier slid out from under his fingers, dumping him rudely, still trapped inside. He dismissed any thought of jumping free; he could not possibly clear the mysterious barrier without a running start, for which he had insufficient room. He glared impotently at the bandits, who sneered back.

"All right, enough fun. Kill the beast." Once again

it was the man on foot who spoke, apparently the group's leader.

The trio moved to obey, but reluctantly; Koros was fully as formidable an enemy as its master. The first raised his lance and urged his horse to a gallop. The warbeast batted aside his charge as a kitten bats a ball of yarn, flinging the man screaming from his horse, his lance snapping against the beast's flank without leaving more than a scratch.

Elmil was awake now, watching helplessly as the other two approached more cautiously, looking for an opportunity to plunge their weapons into the warbeast's vitals. They separated, circling the monster in opposite directions, making it impossible for Koros to face them both; realizing what was happening, the beast went on the offensive and sprang at one of them, claws out, smashing the man off his horse against a rocky hillside. The other flung his spear; it stuck in Koros' shoulder, but failed to slow the beast as it ripped the throat out of the fallen bandit.

"Stop!" cried the apparent leader. "Overman, call off your beast, or I'll kill Elmil!" Elmil looked pleadingly at his quondam captor as the bandit's spear hovered over his heart.

Garth took perhaps half a second to consider, in which time Koros had pounced again, slashing at its remaining attacker without unhorsing him, leaving a bloody corpse to slip slowly from the saddle.

"Down!" Garth roared, and the warbeast suddenly stopped, as docile as a housecat, to tend to its wounded shoulder as best it could, licking at the oozing blood and brushing at the shaft of the spear while keeping a wary eye on the bandit leader.

"Why should I care if Elmil dies?" Both bandit and overman ignored the panic that appeared on Elmil's face as a slight jab kept him from protesting.

"You apparently have some use for a captive."

"No more. I kept him as hostage, but it appears you care as little for him as I do."

The bandit was disconcerted, and hesitated before

saying, "Let us negotiate. Perhaps we can avoid further bloodshed."

"As you wish."

Unsure of himself, the bandit went on. "I fear we have made a mistake in attacking you."

Garth said nothing.

"Therefore, although we have wronged you, we ask that you pardon us, and we will go in peace."

Garth waited before replying, but the bandit could think of nothing further to add; so, finally, the overman said, "You will not bother me again, nor harm my beast."

"You have my word."

"You will leave Elmil alive and in my custody, and receive him back willingly when I free him."

"As you wish."

"You will remove this obstruction, and answer my questions."

"Very well."

"Should you renege on any of these promises, I shall track you down and kill you."

It was the bandit's turn to say nothing.

"Remove this barrier."

Hesitantly, the bandit said, "I must first have your word for my life, and for the lives of my companions . . . if any still survive."

"I give you my word that neither I nor my beast shall slay any of you without further provocation."

"Very well." The bandit turned away and fumbled with something under his vest; Garth felt the air in front of him, and found that the invisible wall was gone. He strode over to where Elmil lay and the bandit leader stood.

"Who are you?"

"I am Dansin of Derbarok."

"You are the leader of the bandits?"

"I was, from the time you slew Khand, our former leader, until now. I do not know if I can be so called any more."

"How did you create that barrier?"

"It is controlled with a talisman given me by the wizard Shang."

"Why did the wizard give you this charm?"

"To subdue you."

"How did Shang know of me?"

"We went to him for aid when you slew our fellows, and told him of the battle, and that you rode toward Mormoreth."

"You could not know whither I rode."

"The road you followed leads only there; the highways to Lagur and Ilnan have been abandoned, and all traffic thither takes other routes."

"So you told Shang of my approach; and then?"

"We asked him for powerful weapons, for magicks to slay you with to avenge our comrades and protect Mormoreth. He refused, saying that such were not necessary to stop a lone adventurer, and that he could not risk letting such as us use them. Instead, he gave us the charm of the invisible wall."

"I would see this charm."

"That was no part of our bargain." The bandit drew back.

"As you will." The overman thought briefly without striking upon any other questions, then said, "Let us see to your fellows." He failed to notice Dansin's surprise when he so readily abandoned his claim to the magical prison.

Fitting actions to words, Dansin, Garth, and Elmil found that of the three other bandits the first was unconscious from his fall but appeared otherwise unhurt, while the other two were quite dead. Next Garth removed the spear from the warbeast's shoulder and treated the wound as best he could. It was not deep, as the point had been embedded in a fold of hide rather than in muscle or bone. The warbeast seemed indifferent to its injuries, save that it licked at each scratch once or twice.

This done, Garth said, "You may take your comrade and go in peace. I ask, however, that you loan Elmil and myself your two extra horses, since you no longer need them. I will return them in Elmil's keeping when I release him."

"Very well." Thus it was arranged, and minutes later Dansin vanished into the darkness, riding his own horse while leading another with the unconscious bandit draped across it, and leaving Garth, Elmil, Koros, two horses and two corpses scattered about the faintly glowing remains of a campfire.

Within minutes, Garth and Elmil were asleep again, while Koros nibbled on one of the corpses.

# CHAPTER FOUR

They awoke late the next day, well after dawn, due to the interruption of their sleep, and were not under way again until almost noon. Now Elmil rode upon one horse, the other carried part of Garth's supplies, and Garth himself rode in comfort astride Koros once more.

The day passed without incident, and their next camp was made at sunset on the edge of the valley of Mormoreth. The towers of the city glittered on the horizon, tall spires of white stone bright against the deepening blue of the eastern sky.

The air was warmer on this side of the mountains as well, and the valley was green and lush with the spring. There were very few trees, as the entire area was farmland; instead, the crops and grasses lay like a thick green carpet in the shadow of the mountains. Garth had rarely seen farms before, being a city-dweller, and never any so rich; the scene was beautiful in a way he had never known before, for in his homeland the only beauties were those of sleek animals, carven stone, and glittering ice. Even in summer the lands were dull and barren, covered only with sparse grass where the overmen's diligent efforts could bring forth no wheat. He had never before seen so much green, nor such a rich shade of green.

However, something looked wrong, even to his untrained eyes; the young corn and wheat did not stand in neat rows, but were scattered about, and grass and weeds grew unchecked amid the crops. These farms were untended and abandoned. He wondered why.

41

He wondered also at the towers of Mormoreth. What were they for? Ordunin had a single tower above the harbor, where a perpetual watch was maintained for the benefit of both the trading ships carrying out furs, ice, carved bone and new-mined gold, and the port itself; the pirates in the region had several times assaulted Ordunin when unsatisfied with their take at sea. The port's other buildings were but one or two stories in height, or at most three; beyond that, stairs became too wearying. But here, amid a vast peaceful valley with land to spare, humans had built a city with a dozen towers, each a good hundred feet in height. Admittedly, the towers were very beautiful as they glowed in the setting sun; the architects had been excellent indeed. But building for beauty alone was something Ordunin could never dream of; mere survival took too much effort.

Contemplating beauty and the significance of beauty, and the further significance of abandoned farmlands, Garth fell asleep, to dream uneasily of the desolate beauties of winter in the Northern Waste, where drifting snow and pinnacles of ice would gleam in the setting sun like the towers of Mormoreth.

The following day Garth awoke once more at dawn, to find Elmil carefully separating his belongings from the overman's. He watched for a moment, then demanded, "What are you doing?"

"I am preparing to wait here while you go to Mormoreth."

"I intend to take you with me."

"I swore never to enter the valley."

"I am compelling you to break that vow."

"I will not."

Garth was momentarily speechless. Until now, Elmil had been a timid creature, with little will of his own. Garth realized he must have underestimated the man's terror of Shang, or else the man's sense of honor. In either case, it hardly seemed worth arguing.

"Very well. I said I would release you, and although I had not intended to do so so soon, I shall. You may go, and take the horses with you."

"Thank you, lord."

Reflecting that he had gotten little use out of his captive and might as well have released him long before rather than wasted food on him, Garth made his own preparations. Shortly thereafter, two very different figures rode in opposite directions from the campsite, Garth astride his warbeast, riding down the overgrown path to the valley, Elmil on horseback, making his way back up the pass into the mountains, leading the other horse.

The sun was warm, and it was not long at all before Garth found himself sweating under his armor. Even the black hair stuffed under his helmet was damp, and his body-fur was matted and sopping. Fur was all very well in colder climates, he told himself, or even in warm weather if one wore nothing else, but with the mail and breastplate trapping the heat, he felt as if he were cooking alive. He considered removing the armor, but did not want to expose himself to attacks from Shang's hirelings and followers, who might easily be lurking hidden in the thick plants alongside the road. He compromised by removing helmet and breastplate, keeping his mail on and perching the helmet on the saddle in front of him where it could be reached and donned in seconds should danger threaten.

It was midafternoon when he neared the city gates, and Garth was moving slowly and cautiously. He was apprehensive, as the untended fields seemed indicative of something very wrong in Mormoreth. He had passed dry and broken irrigation ditches and farmers' cottages standing open and empty. Nowhere had he seen any sign of life. Had he not been told that Shang yet lived and ruled Mormoreth, he would have taken the city to be deserted. Instead, he was forced to assume that the population, probably greatly reduced, somehow managed to survive without ever leaving the city walls. He theorized either vast stockpiles or some magical means of supplying food.

As he approached the walls he saw several small but comfortable-looking stone houses built outside the gate, most likely the homes of farmers and those who dealt closely with farmers—smiths and the like— which also stood abandoned, with open doors and broken windows. Garth was not surprised; it was in keeping with the deserted farms. Undaunted, the over- man rode directly up to the western gate, a huge brass-trimmed wooden portal standing at least fifteen feet in height. The walls themselves were of white marble, clear and unveined and spotlessly clean, that gleamed in the sun. Garth marveled that mere men had built such a thing, and wondered that they had used marble instead of the harder and more common granite. Perhaps the builders had been more concerned with beauty than efficiency, a thought that bothered Garth with its implications of affluence; it was not in keeping with the world as he knew it.

After a brief pause to see if the gatekeeper would admit or challenge him without being hailed, Garth bellowed, "Open!"

His shout echoed faintly from the polished stone walls to either side of the gate, but elicited no other response. After a decent interval, the overman called again, with as little result, and finally for a third time.

When this last shout was met with a renewed si- lence—even the chirping of birds and insects stilled in response to the noise—Garth slid from his mount's back, slipped his breastplate and helmet on and pulled his battle-axe from its boot. Standing braced, his feet well apart, he swung the axe against the weathered wood of the portal.

The blade buried itself in the oak, spraying splinters to either side, but the door did not move. Garth pulled it free and prepared for a second swing, but froze as the sound of laughter trailed down over him from somewhere above.

Stepping back, he looked up to see a figure atop the battlement, a large man who seemed somehow to be in shadow despite the bright sunlight that shown full upon him. With a start, Garth realized that the shadow was in fact the man's skin color, that the man laughing had skin darker than his own, so dark as to be almost black. The overman had not known humans came in such a wide range of hues. He studied this apparition carefully. This curious figure appeared to be well over six feet tall, and Garth guessed his weight at perhaps as much as three hundred pounds; he had an immense barrel chest, a belly to match, and arms and legs as thick as trees. He wore a flowing black robe worked with elaborate gold embroidery; no other ornamentation, no jewelry was to be seen. His face was innocent of any beard, and his hair, as black as the overman's own dead-straight shoulder-length mane, was clipped close to his skull. Garth could see no sword or other weapon in evidence; since no guardsman would be unarmed, this strange man was clearly no ordinary gatekeeper.

The apparition atop the wall was the first to speak.

"Greetings, overman." The voice was deep and resonant, tinged with amusement.

"Greetings, man. I have come in peace. May I enter the city as a friend?"

"So you come in peace? Is it peaceful to bury your weapon in my front door, to hack at my city's defenses?"

"Your pardon, man, but I received no answer to my hail."

"Could you not then accept it that you were not welcome, and go your way?"

"I have business in Mormoreth."

"You have no business in Mormoreth, nor does anyone save myself."

"I regret contradicting you, but I do have business within, the performance of a task set me."

"Ah, a quest! For what?" The voice was plainly mocking now.

"I seek to capture the first living thing I meet in the catacomb beneath the city."

Further laughter greeted this explanation. "Pray,

who set you this impossible task, and for what? Do you seek the hand of some princess? But no, that would not be in keeping with an overman's nature. Wealth, then? Is it for gold you perform this errand?"

"My reasons are my own."

"Oh, come! Who sent you here?"

"I serve one called the Forgotten King, who dwells in Skelleth."

There was absolute silence for a long moment; then, slowly, the man asked, with every trace of humor gone from his voice, "You serve the Forgotten King?"

"So he calls himself."

"Describe him."

Although he wondered why this man, who was apparently Shang himself from his references to "my city," would ask such a thing, Garth responded as best he could. "He is an old man who wears yellow rags. I could not see his hair or eyes when I spoke to him, so I do not know their colors, but he has a long white beard. He is tall and thin, for a human, with—"

"Enough!" The interruption was harsh, as if the speaker were suppressing anger. "Overman, you are unwise. Abandon this quest and have nothing more to do with this . . . this so-called king."

"I have made a bargain."

"Listen, overman, you do not know what you do. Although I have no love for you or your kind, I warn you, I give you my word, that only destruction can come of serving this man."

"I gave my word that I would serve him." Although Garth's voice betrayed no emotion, Shang's words worried him; he wondered just what goals the Forgotten King was pursuing.

"Then argument of your master's treachery will not sway you? Let me warn you then, that your task is impossible. There is but one living thing in the crypts; the king-lizard, known as a basilisk."

Garth had never heard the word. He asked, "What manner of beast is a basilisk, that its capture is impossible?"

"Ah, I forgot; overmen know little of human legends. The basilisk is no natural beast, but the Lord of Reptiles, and the most venomous creature known to science or sorcery. Its breath slays instantly; to touch it is to die; to meet its gaze will turn a man—or overman—to stone. Should one somehow approach within reach and strike it with sword or spear, its poison runs up blade or shaft to kill the wielder before he can pierce its armored hide. It exists only as a result of the blackest magic and serves the Death-God himself. No, overman, you cannot capture this beast and carry it hence, and it can only be fatal to try."

"Nevertheless, I am sworn to do so."

"Fool! Why? What incentive is there, that you give up your life to serve a man, one not even of your own species?"

"I have made a bargain."

"But . . . overman, what is it you are to receive in turn? I am myself a powerful wizard; perhaps we could strike a better bargain."

"It was a trusted oracle that sent me to the one I serve; and though your words sound sincere, I cannot put more trust in you than in the oracle." Garth honestly regretted the truth of his statement; Shang's obvious concern contributed to his own growing discomfiture.

"Very well. Fool that you are, I will let you seek your destruction. But be warned, overman, that should you somehow contrive to succeed, I shall slay you myself. Neither I nor indeed any other can afford to risk allowing the so-called Forgotten King to obtain the basilisk's venom; he could use such a poison to work magicks like none known for centuries; he could cause limitless destruction. Much of my own magic derives from scrapings of floors the basilisk has walked upon. To give the monster itself to the King in Yellow is utter insanity."

"It is not my concern what he does with it; I am merely to bring it to him."

"Then die, like the fool you are, in the attempt. I

will neither aid nor hinder you. Although ordinarily I would slay you merely for having trespassed upon my valley, I do not care to become involved in your doom. If the Forgetten King has indeed sent you here to die, I will not help him by killing you."

"As you will; then open the gates, that I may make my attempt."

"Oh, no; I have just said that I will not aid in your destruction."

Garth snarled in annoyance at this petty delay. He raised his axe and hacked again at the gate as Shang vanished from atop the wall. Splinters flew and he struck repeatedly, until at last he had chopped a hole big enough for him to squeeze through. He did so, and once inside he unbarred and opened the ruined gate to admit Koros; the beast had stood impassively throughout the assault on the portal, and now strode into the city with its usual smooth, graceful gait.

Replacing his axe in its place on the saddle, Garth flexed his arms to remove the tenseness as he looked about at the city of Mormoreth. He and his beast stood in a small plaza, perhaps a hundred feet across, its sides lined with merchants' stalls, with a street opening from the center of each side, save where the gate occupied one. The merchants' stalls were as empty and deserted as the farms Garth had passed outside the city, and the three streets were also uninhabited. An unnaturally complete silence hung over the scene. The overman's footsteps on the packed dirt of the market and the snuffling of the warbeast were the only sounds.

Curious, Garth crossed to one of the abandoned stalls and saw that the goods the owner had hoped to sell still lay spread out for the customer's inspection, a thin layer of dust hiding the details of the embroidered cloths. In the next booth an assortment of pins, needles, and bodkins lay strewn about in disarray, while a statue stood almost lost in the shadowy interior, a life-size figure of a man seated cross-legged, with dust obscuring the folds of the carven garments.

Leaving this unprofitable investigation, Garth led Koros into the street directly opposite the shattered gate, and proceeded cautiously deeper into the city.

The buildings, although dusty and falling into disrepair, were beautiful and well built, mostly of the same white marble as the city walls. Although most were two or three stories in height, Garth could see three of the dozen towers he had admired from across the valley, but still saw no indication of their purpose. Elaborate fountains, now dry and silent, and gardens and planters, now dead and brown from lack of watering, were common; the homes and shops were graceful and elegant even now. Innumerable statues stood on balconies, beside doorways, in gardens, even placed apparently at random in the streets, or blocking doorways; such a profusion of statuary seemed the only lapse in the exquisite taste of the city's inhabitants. Garth wondered once again what had become of them. Had Shang slaughtered them all?

Investigating more closely the oddly scattered sculpture, Garth saw that all were of an amazing lifelikeness; were it not for the uniform gray of the stone, many could be mistaken for living people. Nor were they limited to the usual gracefully posed noblemen of most Orûnian art; the statues represented merchants, housewives, farmers, and children. Glancing down a side-street, the overman saw a cluster that represented gaudily clad young women whose lowcut dresses and curled hair clearly marked them as ladies of pleasure—as Garth knew from his stay in Skelleth. Ordunin, of course, had no need for such, overmen being what they were.

The unbroken stillness was unsettling. Further, Garth realized that he had no idea where an entrance to the crypts might be found. To search the entire city for one could easily take weeks, and although Garth himself had no objection to such a delay, he knew that

Koros would be hungry again in a day or two, and that it was most unlikely it would find game in a valley of farmland. Having no wish to risk letting the monster go hungry, Garth had no intention of resorting to a systematic search; instead, he determined to find an inhabitant and question him or her. Surely Shang had not wiped out everyone!

Upon brief reflection, Garth decided that the most likely place to find either living people or other useful indications was in one of the towers. Thus he entered the nearest, to be confronted with a sight that confirmed what he had subconsciously suspected but refused to admit. Seated in a chair, poised over a table as if to eat, with spoon in hand, sat another perfect statue. The only questions remaining were whether it had been Shang, the basilisk, or some hideous mesalliance of the two that had turned the people of Mormoreth to stone, and whether any had escaped.

Appalled, Garth explored further. It was as he gazed sadly at a child, petrified while clutching a doll that had remained untransformed, that he heard a noise.

He froze. Again he heard it. The sound was in the street outside, and approaching. Moving as quietly as he knew how, Garth crossed to the nearest window; he was still on the ground floor. He peered cautiously out, and to his astonishment saw a man approaching; the astonishment was not so much that a man was walking the streets of Mormoreth, but that Garth recognized him. It was Dansin, the bandit.

Seeing in the bandit leader as good a source of information as he was likely to find, Garth sprang through the window, scattering shattered glass across the street. Before Dansin could do anything but start in surprise at the noise, he found the overman's drawn sword at his throat.

"Man, I would know where to find an entrance to the crypts."

Dansin stammered, "What crypts?" His hand crept toward his vest, but Garth moved faster, and drew forth an intricately carved wooden rod, perhaps an inch in diameter and a foot long.

"I take it this is the device you used to imprison me at our last encounter. How does it work?"

"I . . . you swore not to harm me."

"I swore I would not kill you; nor shall I. However, should you refuse me, you will lose your right hand at the wrist. I want two things: the location of the crypt entrance, and the means of using this talisman."

"I know nothing of any crypt, I swear by the Fifteen!"

"You do know how to use this rod."

"Yes."

"Then explain it."

With much hesitation, the bandit did so; it was worked by pressing various of its carved surfaces in certain sequences. Garth kept Dansin within reach while he tested this information, and was gratified to find it accurate.

"Very good, thief. Now, why are you in Mormoreth?"

"I came to warn Shang of our defeat and your approach."

"How did he respond to your warning?"

"He laughed; he said he would meet you at the gate, and permitted me to stay, so that you would not meet me on the road. Then but an hour ago he returned to the palace in a rage and ordered me thence."

"Very well, then; you may go your way." Garth sheathed his sword, and in an instant Dansin was fleeing toward the gate as if pursued by demons.

Garth watched him go, then turned his own steps in the opposite direction. He had now been reminded that Shang dwelt in the palace. Further, Shang had admitted that he derived much of his magic from the presence of the basilisk. Therefore, it seemed likely that there was an entrance to the catacombs somewhere in or near this palace. If the palace in question were the only one in the city, which it appeared to be from the manner in which it was referred to, then in all likelihood it lay in the center of the city, there being no high ground in this flat-bottomed valley. Thus, Garth headed for the center of the city.

He called for his beast, and Koros appeared from the alley in which Garth had left him. Leading the monster, he strolled on at a casual pace, mulling over possible plans for invading the palace without again confronting Shang.

# CHAPTER FIVE

Before he had gone very far, Garth sighted his objective. The street he was on was very nearly straight, an oddity in human cities, with only a single curve in it perhaps a mile from the gate. After rounding this bend, the overman found himself looking down a broad avenue that opened into a large square. On the far side of the square, its door directly in line with Garth's gaze, was a large and well-made structure some three stories in height, built of gleaming white stone, like most of Mormoreth, and which was plainly the palace that Shang had appropriated. It was still perhaps a quarter mile distant. Garth paused to consider his approach. It was clearly impossible to attempt any kind of stealth with Koros in tow, so he led the beast into a convenient forecourt, out of sight of the square, and tied it loosely to a hitching post; he was well aware that the rope would scarcely begin to restrain the monster if it wanted to leave, but it would serve to reinforce his verbal instruction to stay. He could only hope and trust that he would be back before Koros got hungry enough to disobey him.

Leaving it standing there placidly, still saddled and loaded in case a rapid departure was necessary, he gathered what he thought he might need and proceeded as quietly as he could down the shadowy side of the avenue. His supplies consisted of his broadsword, his dirk, his battle-axe, and a sack containing ropes, chains, hooks, and two shaving mirrors appropriated from dead bandits after his first encounter

with Elmil's band, in addition to the two magical
talismans he had acquired and such staples as purse,
canteen, and a wallet of provisions. In his belt were
flint and steel as well as a prepared torch.

Reaching the corner where the avenue met the
square, Garth looked about. The open area was clearly
a marketplace, with taverns and inns standing dark
and vacant on all sides, the canopies and tents of
various merchants scattered in the dust before him.
It was a good fifty yards square, perhaps more. The
dusty and disarrayed awnings and such numbered
in the dozens.

Almost the entire opposite side was occupied by a
single building: the palace, glistening white marble
that remained spotless despite the city's current de-
populated condition. It had a single great door in the
middle of its façade, a gem-encrusted expanse of beaten
gold at the top of three steps of some rich red stone;
the ground floor had no windows or ornaments except this portal, set in the smooth, blank marble.

Upper stories were another matter; half a dozen
evenly spaced slits served as windows for the second
floor, while the third had a dozen broad casements
of elaborately leaded glass. The gently sloping roof
was edged with innumerable gargoyles, carved of the
same white marble as the walls.

Garth studied the situation. Shang was in there
somewhere, presumably, but the structure was large
enough that most of its interior would undoubtedly be
out of sight and sound of the door. Unless the wizard
were lying in wait for him, the odds were he could
simply walk in the front door unnoticed—unless there
were some sort of alarm. If there were, he would hear
it, and could simply turn around and walk out again.

Although the boldest course, this was also the sim-
plest, and therefore most likely the best; he had no
way of knowing where in the palace he might encounter the wizard, so one point of entry was as good
as another, making it foolish to risk climbing in windows where he could easily slip and break his neck.

His course of action decided, Garth strode across the square, dodging the collapsed tents. The sun, setting somewhere over his right shoulder, glittered redly on the gems that studded the palace door. Marching up the three steps, he grasped the handle and pushed; nothing happened. He pushed harder; the door still refused to yield. He could see no sign of lock or bar, yet it gave no more than would a mountainside; either the palace had been designed to withstand a siege or there was sorcery at work here. In either case, Garth did not care to press the issue. He considered trying to cut through the door with his axe as he had the city gate, but he rejected the idea. If anything would annoy Shang, the ruination of his front door would. Furthermore, the noise attendant upon such a proceeding would be vastly greater than that of his intended surreptitious entry, so that even if the wizard were in the far corner of the palace he might hear it.

Therefore another entrance must be found. Garth descended the red stone steps and turned right, to make a circuit of the building. This led him through a rather malodorous alleyway perhaps six feet in width, where he found the south face of the palace to be as totally blank and featureless on all three floors as the front was on the first. Then, some forty yards along, he found himself in a broader, more wholesome street at right angles to the alleyway. The back of the palace, he saw, had the same casements and gargoyles at top, the same slits on the second floor, the same smooth façade at ground level, save that where the golden door was in the front, the back had a large arch, perhaps fifteen feet wide and a dozen high, filled with an oaken gate.

A brief attempt showed that this barrier was as solidly closed as was the golden portal, if not more so, and the arguments against hacking it down still held; so Garth continued to the northern face, into an alleyway of perhaps eight-foot width, which was almost black in the gathering twilight. Here the palace was again utterly blank and featureless.

Emerging once more into the market-square, Garth realized that daylight was fading rapidly and that he could not afford to waste much more time if he wanted to be able to see what he was doing; therefore he discarded his consideration of such possibilities as concealed doorways, lock-picking, tunnels from adjacent buildings, and other unlikely means of ingress, and set his mind to reaching the third-floor windows . . . One, he could see, was not closed completely; perhaps an inch separated the metal casement from its frame.

A single attempt convinced him that the palace walls were not readily scalable; the smooth marble provided no hand- or toe-holds, nor did he care to waste time and energy noisily making such holds with his axe. He did not care to attempt lassoing or grappling a gargoyle and clambering up the rope, because he doubted either the gargoyles or the rope were strong enough to hold him, and knew that he was no expert at either throwing or climbing ropes. No, the best approach, he saw, would be to get onto the roof somehow and lower himself down to the window from above, with two or three lengths of rope securely fastened to whatever could be found.

Since the palace itself was unscalable, he would have to get onto the roof from one of the adjacent buildings; to the right was an inn some three stories high, almost as tall as the palace, with overhanging eaves that Garth doubted he could get past, while to the left stood a house of two stories, the upper floor overhanging the lower so that its roof ended not more than two yards from the palace wall and perhaps ten feet below the level of the palace roof. That might serve as a jumping-off point, though the jump itself would be a difficult one.

Reaching that first roof, however, would be easy; an unfallen merchant's canopy sloped away from the house, supported by a fairly substantial wooden frame. Without further consideration, Garth grabbed the lower edge of the canopy, mere inches above his head. Moving as quickly as he could, he swung himself up onto it. The cloth gave, straining dangerously, and a cloud of dust arose, making his eyes water, but the canopy held—at first. He scrambled rapidly up the sloping homespun, feeling it give as he did so; the cloth was tearing loose from its framework. He rolled sideways onto the cloth-covered wood, only to hear the frame creak and feel it start to sag under his weight; but then he was at the top, clinging to the rough façade of the house. It was not rough enough for a proper hold, however, and he knew his grip was insufficient to save him if the rickety canopy were to collapse. Although the fall would probably not hurt him, it would ruin his planned approach to the palace, as well as make a considerable and undesirable racket.

He waited for the swaying and creaking to subside, spreading his weight as best he could, as he considered his next move. The eaves would be within easy reach if he were to stand up, but such an action would undoubtedly bring the tattered merchant's stall down in complete ruin. Perhaps if he could get a toe into the wall of the house he could let that carry the strain; there was an opening between two badly cut stones almost an inch high and four inches long. Carefully, slowly, he brought his left leg up and wedged the pointed toe of his boot into the flaw.

Thus anchored, he pulled himself up the wall a few inches at a time, his right leg resting on the wooden frame, until he was kneeling, his left leg braced against the wall, his hands, with all four thumbs digging in, clinging to the wall above his head. Then, in a single sudden surge, he flung himself upward, catching himself with his arms up over the eaves almost to his shoulder, then swinging his leg up onto the roof. From that perch he pulled up his other leg as he saw the canopy frame below him pull loose from the wall and slowly, quietly fall to the ground, the cloth forming a sort of parachute that both broke the fall and muffled the inevitable clatter.

He paused briefly to catch his breath but dared not wait, lest Shang had heard the noise; the collapse could have been caused by wind or wear, but Garth still had to get out of sight. Wasting no time in preparation, he stood and ran for the roof-edge facing the palace, and launched himself into the short gap between buildings. His run had been hindered by the slope of the roof and he had not fully caught his breath after gaining the rooftop, so the leap was short and sloppy, but his outstretched fingers reached one of the projecting gargoyles and wrapped around it automatically. To his surprise, the carving held; he had underestimated the local masons.

Carefully, he worked his fingers up across the stone until his hold was less precarious; then he swung his feet forward to press against the smooth white marble of the palace wall and give him sufficient traction to shift his grip, so that he could once again swing a leg up. This time it took two attempts to hook a toe over the parapet behind the grinning sculptures; Garth blamed it on the rapidly fading twilight rather than admit that he was tiring already. He was not as young as he once was, having lived more than a century. Though overmen could anticipate a lifespan of about two hundred years, Garth had long since lost the first bloom of youthful vigor.

Having finally gained the security of the palace roof, he moved well back from the edge, out of sight of the market-square if he kept his head down, and rested. Looking about him, he realized that the palace, which he already knew to be almost square, was a hollow square; a large courtyard occupied its center. Though he could not be seen from the market, he was in plain view of a third-floor open gallery that ran the length of the courtyard's opposite side. He crouched lower instinctively, though he knew that there was nowhere on the roof he could conceal himself completely; even the various chimneys were low, little more than holes in the roof. He lay motionless, waiting for a sound that would indicate Shang's whereabouts.

None came.

He remained where he was for several minutes, considering his best course of action. It would be much easier to enter the palace by dropping down into the courtyard or lowering himself into one of the galleries or balconies that adorned it, than by climbing in the front window. In ordinary circumstances it would also be less likely to be noticed. However, circumstances in Mormoreth were far from ordinary; the city was apparently uninhabited except for Shang, and Shang lived in the palace. Therefore, it was quite possible that at any given time he might be on a balcony, in a gallery, or strolling the courtyard, perhaps where he could watch Garth's descent while Garth was unable to see him until it was too late. On the other hand, an approach to the front window would be visible only from the marketplace and the room immediately inside. Shang was not in the marketplace, and could be seen and avoided if he were; and the odds against his presence in a single room on an upper floor were much better than the odds on the courtyard. Garth's original plan of action was still clearly the best.

Reaching into his pack, he brought out three ropes. He looped one around one of the low chimneys, and tied it as best as he could in the gathering darkness—which also recommended the front window, as glimmers of reflected firelight, presumably from torches and lamps, could be discerned in the courtyard, while a careful peering over the gargoyles showed the open window to be dark. A second rope was placed around a gargoyle, Garth's faith in them having been increased; and the third rope, since no other anchorage was available, was tied to the head of another gargoyle adjacent to the first, just behind the thing's batlike ears—it had no neck.

The three ropes were loosely braided together, and lowered carefully over the edge; then Garth lowered himself and climbed cautiously onto the dangling cord. To his relief it held, showing no signs of undue strain.

Once below the level of the carvings, it was a simple matter to reach out, swing the casement open—it was well-oiled and swung freely without squeaking—and hook his legs over the sill. Then he was inside, sliding the rope carefully back over his shoulder so that it would not slap noisily against the wall. He regretted the necessity of leaving it dangling there, but with any sort of luck at all it would remain unnoticed until morning. Garth hoped to be out of the palace, his task done, by morning.

The room he found himself in was an unused bedchamber; a vast canopied four-poster occupied most of one wall, while directly opposite stood an ornately carved wardrobe and an elegant full-length mirror. Tapestries covered all the walls, divided here and there to allow draperied doorways. There was only the single window.

Moving carefully around the room counterclockwise, Garth peered carefully through each doorway. The first led to an indoor privy with a complex array of plumbing, which Garth would have liked to study further but could not by the feeble light available. He considered lighting his torch, but decided it was an unnecessary risk. The second door revealed a storeroom of some sort; the third a hallway; the fourth, which had a line of light surrounding the rectangle of drapery, Garth bypassed temporarily; and the fifth and last led to what was apparently a dressing room, with racks of women's dresses along either side. Returning to the fourth doorway, Garth used all his stealth and caution in peering past the velvet curtain. It took his eyes a few seconds to adjust to the light.

He was looking at another room of approximately the same dimensions as the bedchamber, furnished with a desk and an assortment of chairs and couches —a sitting room, apparently. It was not lit itself, but on the far side a wooden double door stood wide open, revealing many-paned glass doors through which torchlight poured; they apparently opened onto one of the courtyard galleries.

He had two choices: the darkened hallway or the torchlit gallery. The decision was simple; having rejected the courtyard route once, he saw no reason to risk it now.

Cautiously, he slipped past the velvet drape into the darkness of the hallway beyond. He could see almost nothing of his surroundings. There were neither windows nor skylights; the faint trace of light, far too little to be of any use, seeped in from the rooms and chambers to either side. As best the overman could determine, the hallway extended for perhaps a dozen yards from where he stood. At least two other rooms opened off it, detectable from the pale-gray glimmer in the blackness made by their doorways. Inching almost soundlessly, his feet cushioned by rich carpet, Garth moved down the corridor.

When he had passed the last pale seepings of light and worked his way a yard or two into the stygian dark beyond, his forward foot suddenly missed the floor; he was at the head of a staircase. Finding his way entirely by feel now, he moved carefully, step-by-step down the spiral until he emerged, long minutes later, on the ground floor. He had bypassed the intermediate level without hesitation, and only regretted that the stairs did not continue into the cellars, or better still the crypts themselves.

The final step deposited him on soft carpeting again; by the feel of the air and the tiny echoes of the faint rattling of his armor and weapons, he knew himself to be in a large chamber. Although it did not yet seem the proper time to ignite the torch, he decided that it would be appropriate to risk a light; he had a few dry splinters of wood in his belt-pouch, as well as flint and steel, and carefully struck a spark to one of these. It caught almost immediately, to his relief, and smouldered a dull red, casting little light but enough for Garth's purposes.

The room he was in was indeed large, and richly

furnished; although he could see little detail, he could
see that the floor was lost beneath overlapping car-
pets, the walls shrouded in tapestries that caught the
light where gold had been woven in, the great
oaken table that stood in the center of the room elaborately carven and its chairs luxuriously upholstered.
The room was apparently a dining chamber of some
sort. Heavy wooden shutters covered what Garth decided must be openings into the courtyard, most likely
equipped with outer doors of glass like the ones he
had seen upstairs. A cavernous fireplace occupied the
far end of the chamber, and to his left two large
wooden doors led, presumably, to other parts of the
palace. It was under the nearer of these portals that a
light suddenly sprang up. Instantly Garth dropped his
glowing twig and crushed it underfoot while reaching
for his sword hilt with his other hand. He waited as
footsteps sounded dimly through the closed door, approaching slowly and casually. When they paused he
realized he was holding his breath, and let it out carefully. There came the sound of a cabinet opening, the
sound of its latch and the squeal of its hinges too high-
pitched for a full-sized door. Something was moved
about, then the cabinet was closed again. Through
this Garth stood motionless, alert and ready for whatever should happen. At last the footsteps sounded
again, retreating this time. The light grew dimmer,
then went out, leaving Garth once again in utter darkness.

Slowly, the overman relaxed. That was as close as
he cared to come to being discovered by Shang. He
considered his next move carefully; he knew that
Shang made use of the basilisk's venom in some way,
from the wizard's own words, and he had just heard
him either obtain something from storage or restore
it to its place. Therefore it did not seem unlikely that
the next room was where the basilisk venom was
kept, for what could the wizard be moving about
other than magical apparatus? Also, what point would
there be in storing such a dangerous commodity fur-

ther than necessary from its source? Quite possibly
the entrance to the catacombs lay very near, beyond
the door he now faced. If not, it was not unreasonable
to think that a clue to where that entrance did lie
might be found with the basilisk venom. It seemed
plain that that room bore investigating. Shang had
just visited it, and so would presumably not return
immediately—though he might, of course; care was
necessary—so that time should not be wasted. His
decision made, Garth crossed to the doorway, finding
his way by touch and memory, and groped for the
door-handle. He found it and worked the latch. The
door began to swing open of its own accord. It had
apparently been hung badly. However, since it swung
silently, Garth made no move to stop it; instead he
stepped through when the opening was wide enough.
After a moment's thought, he caught the door and
swung it closed again, catching the latch and lowering
it soundlessly in place; although this cut off one possible route of retreat, or at least put a delay in it, that
seemed less important than leaving such an obvious
proof of his presence should Shang investigate this
room while Garth was elsewhere.

The room he was in was dark, though not so black
as the dining hall; traces of light slipped in under
half a dozen closed doors on two sides of the chamber
and shuttered windows on a third. He was apparently
very near indeed to that portion of the palace Shang
used for his personal quarters. Garth's eyes were already adjusted to the dark; after closing the door and
turning away from the lit cracks, he had little difficulty in discerning the contents of the room. He
immediately realized how wrong his assumptions had
been.

He was in a kitchen; Shang had merely been obtaining a snack. One wall was lined with cupboards
and cabinets, with an open arch in their midst that
must lead to the larder and pantry. Around a corner
must be the scullery, to judge from the pans that lay
near. One wall was taken up mostly with assorted

ovens and a huge open hearth. Tables and counters were scattered around, and the air smelled of vegetables and cooked meat.

Garth accepted his error with a shrug; he should have expected the next room to a dining hall to be a kitchen, and he had not. It was a mistake, but it was past and would not be made again. He was where he was, and would have to make the best of it. In fact, he told himself, this was a good place to be. The crypts were, of course, under the palace; therefore the palace cellars were a likely place to find an entrance, and the kitchen was the natural place to find an entrance to the cellars. Unquestionably one, or maybe several, of the many doors opened on stairs to the cellars. The only question was, which door?

Well, it was a safe assumption that the cellars were not illuminated at the moment, which eliminated from consideration those doors that showed light; that left three doors in the main portion of the kitchen, and perhaps others in the pantries and scullery.

He began to inch his way across the room toward the nearest of the unlit doors. His boots scraped slightly on the flagstone floor, so he switched to slow, careful strides, lifting his feet straight up, advancing them, and placing them gingerly down. He was perhaps halfway across the darkened kitchen when his moving foot collided in midstride with a kettle that lay on its side where it had been flung by Shang—who was rather a sloppy housekeeper. The copper pot rolled aside, rattling, when the toe of his foot struck it; he was thrown off balance and caught himself only at the cost of a loud thud as his foot hit the floor and his hand grabbed at a nearby table. He froze.

The kettle had scarcely stopped rolling when he heard the wizard's approaching footsteps. His right hand fell once again to his sword, while his left slipped inside his cloak, seeking the pocket where he had put the so-called Jewel of Blindness, as he told himself that if ever he needed magical aid it was now.

Groping, he found the pocket; he did not dare take

his eyes from the general direction of the lit doorways, as he had no way of knowing which one was about to burst open and admit Shang. Being unaware from what direction the attack was to come, he could not afford to be looking the wrong way when it arrived. His three fingers fumbled about, his thumbs hooked over the pocket's edge to catch anything that fell. He felt the hard lump of the gem, and started to draw it forth.

A door slammed open, flung back against the wall. The wizard stood framed in the doorway, a black silhouette against the torchlit room beyond. Garth was blinded momentarily by the sudden light, but none-theless his sword was drawn and ready by the time the door had stopped its abrupt movement; his left hand was also held out before him, the Jewel of Blindness clutched tightly in his fist.

To his astonishment, Shang ignored him; he said nothing, made no threatening move. Instead he peered into the gloomy kitchen as a drunkard would peer into an empty bottle, as if he had expected and wanted to see something that wasn't there.

Not yet accepting his good fortune, Garth held his breath and stood ready, the slow realization that something was wrong seeping into his brain; he could not see the end of his sword, which should be well within his field of vision. Had he drawn the dirk by mistake? No, the weight difference would have told him of his error. He looked down, to be suddenly overwhelmed with a most peculiar form of vertigo; he could not see his hands, nor his legs, nor any other portion of his body or attire; his sword was as invisible as air. It was a very strange and unsettling experience, as if he were somehow adrift in midair; yet his other senses told him that he still stood with his feet firmly on the ground, with sword in hand.

# CHAPTER SIX

Shang stood in the doorway for a long moment, staring into the seemingly empty darkness. Then, with a shrug, he stepped back a pace and reached to one side, his hand disappearing around the doorframe to reappear almost immediately, clutching the stub of a torch. Casually, as if he had dismissed the possibility of an ambush, the wizard strolled into the kitchen and looked about. Seeing the kettle where it lay by Garth's now-invisible boot, he crossed the room, picked it up, and placed it on the table with a slight frown. Garth stood utterly unmoving, not even daring to breathe for fear he should be detected somehow. The wizard's hand passed within a few inches of his foot, and the overman wondered what would happen should Shang touch him. Elmil had said the jewel rendered the user invisible, inaudible, and intangible; then would the wizard's hand pass through him? Would he feel it? Would it harm him?

He had no opportunity to find out, as Shang did not happen to touch him. Instead, the thaumaturge, after restoring the kettle to its place, used his bit of torch to light a hanging oil lamp, then tossed the stub into the fireplace, where it was lost amid a shower of gray ash. The lamp flared up brightly for an instant, then subsided to a smoky and malodorous glow as Shang began opening and rummaging in various cabinets; he placed a plate of cheese on the table beside the kettle, then continued, apparently searching for something. Finally, with a noise of disgust, he slammed the last cabinet and crossed to a door, the same door

66

Garth had planned to try. In the flickering lamplight the overman noticed that a heavy padlock held the door shut. He carefully considered, as quickly as he could, what this could signify; why would one door be locked when others were not? It guarded something valuable—perhaps the crypts, where the basilisk lived?

He had no time for further thought, as Shang turned a massive key in the lock and swung the door open; if he was to get inside that door, speed was essential. He ran through the door a fraction of a second before the wizard himself stepped casually through, pulling it shut behind him.

Unfortunately, the door opened on a narrow landing at the head of a staircase. Garth lost his balance as a result of his mad dash and stumbled awkwardly halfway down the long flight before he managed to grasp to rail and halt his headlong progress. To his astonishment, he felt no bumps or bruises from his numerous impacts with both stairs and railing, nor did he make a sound; the silence was, in fact, rather eerie and horrible, as if he no longer really existed.

As the door slammed, shutting off the dim light from the kitchen, a bright little flame suddenly flashed into being; Garth saw with a curious mixture of fear and fascination that it came directly from the wizard's finger. Shang used it to light a torch that stood ready in a bracket above the landing, then extinguished it with a gesture and picked up the much brighter torch.

Looking around, Garth saw that he was more or less at the midpoint of approximately two dozen steps, hewn of some dull gray stone. On one side of the steps ran a wall of rough blocks of the same stone, while on the other there was a black iron railing to which Garth was clinging. Beyond the railing there extended a sizable wine cellar, with damp stone walls on either side and intricate, ancient stone vaulting overhead, its limits lost in the darkness beyond the torch's glow; in the portion that could be seen stood countless old and bewebbed wine-racks, some full, some empty, some in intermediate states. The light shifted, and Garth turned his gaze upward again to see Shang approaching. Not caring to risk a collision, he backed hastily down the steps, keeping a few paces ahead of the wizard until they both stood at the bottom, where Garth stepped aside and permitted Shang to move unimpeded to the nearest rack of bottles.

As he did, Garth was reprimanding himself for making another unjustified assumption; it was much more natural that Shang would seek a bit of wine to go with his cheese than that he would go prowling un- armed into the catacombs.

As if to confirm that the overman had acted hastily, Shang said loudly, "Ah! Perfect!" He drew forth a cob- webby bottle, dark liquid visible through its murky glass, then turned back toward the stairs. Garth remained where he was, attempting to plan his next move.

Although Shang's visit to the cellar had been in no way connected with the crypts, it was still perfectly possible that an entrance was to be found somewhere amid the wine-racks; since Garth was already down here it would do no harm to check. Therefore he would let the wizard leave, investigate, and then leave himself if he found nothing. It was only when he heard the padlock clicking back into place that he realized he had forgotten about it. He would either have to wait until the wizard was thirsty again or use his axe to hack open the door when it came time to depart. He felt rather foolish.

However, since there was nothing he could do about it, he would make the best of the situation and carry on with his intention of searching the cellar. Fortu- nately, Shang had not bothered to douse the torch, but had merely stuck it back in its bracket, still lit. Garth wondered if this meant he would be returning shortly. Presumably he would be, in order to restock the wine-cupboards in the kitchen. Therefore it would be advisable to work quickly, so as to have the torch back into its holder when Shang should return. Garth decided he could count on only as much time as it took a man to drink a rather small bottle of wine, which left no time for delay. He hurried up the steps and reached up to take the torch from its place. He closed his fingers around it and tugged. It did not move. Startled, he pulled again; again, the torch remained as motionless as the cellar wall. Garth removed his hand, then replaced it and tried again; still the wood refused to budge. Perhaps it was enchanted? It seemed rather unlikely that the wizard would bother with ensorcelling a torch in a wine cellar. Perhaps his invisible fingers were in the wrong place, and he was trying to move the bracket? But no, he distinctly felt the rough grain of the wood.

Studying his invisible hand, a horrible thought suddenly struck him: where was his sword? He felt where its hilt should be, and found nothing; his left hand still clutched the Jewel of Blindness, but his right hand had been empty since he staggered on the stairway and grabbed at the railing. He must have dropped the weapon, either in the kitchen or on the stairs; he could see no trace of it. Either it was still invisible, or it lay now on the kitchen floor as clear proof of his presence. It occurred to him that it was very well indeed that it had been the sword he had dropped, rather than the gem, which was his only means of restoring himself to visibility. To avoid any risk of losing it as well, he carefully tucked it into a pouch at his belt, a rather tricky proceeding while invisible. With both hands free, he then reached up and grasped the torch again, carefully feeling its shaft where it met the iron bracket. He could detect no latch or other impediment. He applied his full strength, which should have torn the entire bracket from its mountings; the torch did not so much as flicker. Either it was indeed enchanted, or this was some side effect of his intangible state . . . probably the latter. After all, could intangibles such as fear or courage lift a torch from its resting place? He descended the stairs once more and chose a bottle at random; he could not budge it, any more than he could lift the torch. Likewise, he realized, even if he found the door to the crypts, he would be unable to open it. Well, he decided, such details were best left until actually encountered. He was unsure he would be able to resume his invisibility once he broke it—assuming he could break it—and did not care to abandon his best protection against discovery until the last possible moment.

He wondered again what had become of his sword; wherever it was, it was apparently still invisible, or else Shang would have come back seeking him upon finding it on the kitchen floor. It struck him that he would have heard it fall, ordinarily; the inaudibility the spell conferred apparently affected the user as well as everyone else. In trial, he attempted to shout, and discovered he could not hear himself do so. No wonder the bandits had been so disorganized in their attack; it was a wonder they had been as well grouped as they were. The result of long practice, no doubt. Well, at least he could still feel; the intangibility apparently wasn't that complete.

It was complete enough, though. He couldn't move the torch, so he couldn't very well search the walls with it. He remembered the torch stuck in his belt and, groping, found it; that he could still handle. He drew it forth, climbed the stairs once again, and held it to the flame of the lit one. Nothing happened; no flame appeared. He started to feel for the oiled tip, and burnt his fingers in doing so. It was afire. Naturally, though, the flames were as invisible as the torch, casting invisible light.

Garth found himself wishing he knew the names of some appropriate gods to swear by; profanity seemed the only response in such a situation. Unfortunately, he did not. Like most overmen, he was an atheist, or at least an agnostic, refusing to listen to the babble of competing priesthoods without tangible evidence of the existence of the countless gods and goddesses they espoused. As a result of this widespread attitude, there were no priests of any description to be found in the Northern Waste.

He carefully stamped out the invisible flame with his invisible boot, and caught the odor of invisible smoke. He wondered if Shang would be able to smell his presence. He had no idea how well humans could smell; it would seem that such prominent noses should be fairly sensitive but, recalling the foulness of Skelleth, he decided that the appearance must be deceiving.

It seemed that the only thing to do was to search the walls as best he could in the dim light, working mostly by touch despite his inability to lift so much as a fallen leaf. He could still sense textures, though a silk drapery would give no more than a stone wall under his intangible fingers.

To his surprise, he found that in a way the darkness was comforting; he didn't expect to see his hands or feet in the dark, so their absence was much less distracting than in the light. He found his way without difficulty to the slightly damp and noticeably cool stone wall, and began cautiously feeling his way along, dodging around wine-racks when necessary, and likewise around cobwebs, which were as unbreakable as steel mesh to him now. Enough light trickled through the frames to keep him from actually colliding with anything. The miscellaneous projections he encountered were visible as patches of more complete darkness. No sort of detail could be made out, however; his explorations were of necessity tactile rather than visual.

He gradually became absorbed in his task, noticing and mentally cataloging an intriguing variety of textures in the stone and losing all sense of time. It was only when he reached a corner and decided to take a brief rest that he noticed he was now in complete darkness, even the glow of the torch lost amid the intervening wine-racks. He had systematically explored at least a hundred feet of wall, inch by inch; it must have taken hours, he realized in astonishment, yet Shang had not returned. He had no idea of the time, but guessed that the sun must have risen.

He rose from his comfortable crouch and strode

back toward the far end of the cellar where the stairs were. As he did, he saw that the torchlight was dimmer than before. Breaking into a trot, he arrived at the foot of the stairs and saw that the torch had burnt down to a stub, too short to be held. In a moment it would go out. Further, there was nothing he could do to prevent it. He wondered whether some ill had befallen Shang, or whether he had merely forgotten about fetching more wine. It made little difference. As Garth watched, the flame flickered and died to a dull red glow that slowly faded.

A slight uneasiness touched him briefly, but he shook it off. If something had happened to the wizard, he would have to break the invisibility spell in order to leave the cellar; if he could not break the spell he would be trapped indefinitely. Of course he would not die of thirst, but he thought it doubtful that an overman could live for very long on nothing but wine. It did not occur to him that he would be unable to get at the wine in his intangible state. Also, his mount still waited for him in the city outside; it would be hungry if no one fed it within the next day or so. Well, the warbeast could take care of itself; he had his own worries. He turned his attention back to the cellar walls.

It was a long time later when he finally came across what was undoubtedly a door. The stone ended, there was a wooden frame, and set in a few inches was a wooden panel studded with iron spikes such as were used to discourage trespassers from attempting to break doors in with their shoulders. It was the first trace of anything other than solid stone he had found anywhere in the walls. Investigating further, he felt what were undoubtedly hinges. Although he knew it was useless, he pushed against the opposite edge. It refused to yield. It would seem, he decided, that now was the appropriate time to try and turn himself visible once more. He reached into his belt-pouch and found the gem. Carefully, he tried to pull it out.

It caught; one of it edges had snagged in the pouch's lining.

Annoyed, he tugged at it. At first it held, then suddenly it sprang free and flew out of his grasp. Panic-stricken, Garth fell on his knees and groped for it, but found only dust. Without thinking, he yanked out his flint and steel and tinder and struck a spark, forgetting that the flame and light would be invisible.

The tinder caught and flared a bright yellow in Garth's perfectly normal, visible hands. He snorted with relief as he realized that he had somehow broken the enchantment while fumbling with the gem.

Quickly, before the flickering tinder could die, he pulled out his torch and held it to the flame; the oils, sooty and no longer fresh, took several seconds to catch, but flared up at last in smoky red light.

Pocketing flint and steel with one hand while the other held the torch, Garth saw that he had used the last of his tinder; he could not afford to lose the torch, his only source of light. A glance around showed him that there were other torches, long unused and covered with dust and cobwebs, mounted high along the cellar walls. He lit the nearest one, so as to have a second flame if he lost his first, then systematically collected himself an armload of unlit brands from the other brackets and distributed them about his person. This done, he turned his attention to the door he had found.

It was a massive thing, with three heavy black hinges supporting what appeared to be braced and layered oak, fit to withstand a siege and studded with a myriad of inch-long spikes. It was held shut by a heavy latch, secured with a massive bolt lock—to which Shang undoubtedly held the key.

Reminded of the wizard and his works, he glanced around for the Jewel of Bilndness, but didn't see it. He shrugged. It had served his purpose, and he didn't care to spend the time to search for it; he wanted to get the basilisk above ground before Koros became hungry enough to go hunting. He turned his attention to the latch and lock, holding the torch as close as he could without igniting anything.

The latch was of little consequence; it could be

worked from either side, apparently. The lock was the only difficulty. Nor did he have to worry about bars or locks on the other side, as Shang would be as unable pass them as he—probably. He was unsure as to whether such things could be manipulated magically. There was the possibility of a protective spell of some sort, but he would deal with that if it became necessary and not before.

The door fit its frame reasonably well, but close scrutiny revealed a narrow crack an inch or two above the lockbolt; through it Garth could see light glinting on the shiny metal of the bolt itself, proof that it had been recently worked and the rust scraped off. Putting aside the torch, he drew his dirk and found that the narrow blade fit into the opening. He forced it down until he felt it scrape on the bolt, then pried sideways, moving the bolt a fraction of an inch. He repeated this several times. Then, while holding the dagger-tip where it was, he peered into the crack. He could not be certain, but the bolt appeared to have moved perceptibly and not slid back completely. He continued; with a dozen more prying motions something snapped, and his dagger sprang free. He saw, to his disgust, that the point had broken off; however, a careful study of the crack seemed to show that the broken tip had worked its way between the lock and the frame. With the blunted end of the blade he pried once more.

There was a loud click, a sort of "thunk", and the lock was open.

Working the latch, Garth pushed on the door. It gave, slowly, with a harsh scratching sound where the tip of his dagger was wedged between the lock and the frame. He pressed harder, and it swung abruptly open, precipitating him forward into the darkness beyond.

He tumbled awkwardly down a few steps, then caught himself. He was on a narrow stair which descended further than he could see by the dim torch-light, with walls of solid stone on either side. The walls, in fact, appeared to be natural uncut stone; he could

see no seams or mortar. The tunnel and stair were
hewn from the living bedrock of the valley.

A breath of cool air wafted up to him from the
invisible depths below. He had found the crypts of
Mormoreth, he was quite certain.

Caution was called for from here on; at any moment
he might encounter the basilisk. His only means of
ensuring that he would not be petrified in such an
encounter was the shaving mirrors he had brought,
taken from the dead bandits. He found one of the two
mirrors in his pack and stood it on his shoulder, holding
it in place with his free hand. Then he turned his head
and angled the mirror so that he could see the reflection of the descending steps in it, and twisted his helmet
around on his head so that its earpiece blocked his
view. As long as he looked toward the mirror he would
be unable to see in front of him, except by reflection.
It was an awkward and uncomfortable arrangement,
but he thought it would probably do.

Thus equipped, he returned to the head of the staircase, retrieved his torch, and pushed the door to, being
careful not to let it lock. He returned his broken dirk
to its sheath, then turned and descended, holding the
torch high and finding his way entirely by the image in
the mirror.

# CHAPTER SEVEN

The stairs curved somewhat back and forth, with a
sinuous grace; they continued downward for perhaps a
hundred steps, perhaps more, and ended in a small
chamber with a corridor opening from each side. The
air was cool and dry, free of any movement or breeze.
Garth had lost his sense of direction on the long,
curving staircase, but that mattered little so far under-
ground.

The corridor walls were astonishingly clean; there
was no dust, and not a cobweb to be seen. Likewise,
the antechamber was completely empty, nothing but a
stark cube of stone with three corridors and the staircase opening from its four sides. There were no stalac-
tites, nor niter deposits, nor any other sign of age, of
growth, or of decay. It was as if the tunnels were newly
bored. Still, there was an indefinable something, perhaps a scent in the air, which made the overman
suspect that the catacombs were very ancient indeed,
ancient and somehow evil. Certainly they were totally
silent; there was no dripping water, no rustle of mice,
no scratching insects, and the silence seemed somehow
oppressive and ominous.

Moving slowly and carefully, guiding himself by the
dim reflections in his shoulder-mirror, Garth advanced
up the left-hand corridor and started his search for a
living thing. He had hoped that despite Shang's warning he might somehow find some minor vermin, perhaps a fly or a rat, before coming across the basilisk;
but having seen the utterly dead and sterile corridors,
he all but gave up on that idea. His footsteps echoed
from the blank walls like the booming of a drum, and

he was quite sure that the buzzing of a gnat or the swish of a lizard would be magnified to audible proportions if such a thing dwelt anywhere nearby. He began to wonder how it was that he could not hear anything of the basilisk.

As he proceeded, moving through the complex web of corridors, Garth began to realize that he should have brought a thread to find his way out by; the crypts were a labyrinth of branching tunnels, echoing chambers, subtly sloping floors and identical passages which might well have been designed to confuse an intruder. He wondered what their original purpose had been, but could think of nothing plausible.

As time passed he began to feel strangely tired, and perhaps a trifle nauseous. He shook his head to clear it, and paused in his patrol. In so doing, he noticed that the echoes of his footsteps could still be heard, resounding and reechoing, for long seconds after he stopped.

Why was he tired and ill? True, he had not slept in a day or two, but that was not unusual, and he had always been able in the past to go without sleep for as much as a week without difficulty. Perhaps it was hunger? He found a strip of dried meat in his pack and devoured it; it made no difference. In doing so, however, he noticed a peculiar smell, and realized that it had been present for some time and growing steadily stronger. It was a dry, reptilian smell, rather horrible; it could only be the odor of the basilisk, and the monster's poisonous breath was undoubtedly what was weakening him. It meant he was drawing near his goal.

Gathering himself together again, he adjusted his shoulder-mirror and moved on. His progress was necessarily quite slow, navigating by reflection. Still, it was with surprising suddenness that he found himself looking at a low, humped shape that lay resting against the wall of a good-sized chamber. There could be no doubt that this was his quarry.

He took a step further, so that the sleeping shape

was lit by his flickering torch; it was a dark, rich green, some seven feet long, counting the thin, pointed tail, and somehow forbidding in appearance. As he studied its reflected image, it awoke, raised its head and peered at him.

It had golden eyes, slanting, slit-pupiled eyes, eyes that caught Garth's; he froze, and tried to tear his gaze from the mirror. He could not. His eyes were dry; he could not blink. He stared fixedly at the monster's reflected face until his crimson eyes ached. Finally, the creature moved, rising to its feet, and the spell was broken. Garth closed his eyes and held them tightly shut, afraid to meet that baleful gaze again.

The image of the basilisk's eyes remained, even with his eyes shut; those hideous yellow orbs were like nothing Garth had ever seen, deep and hypnotic, tinged with an aura of knowing, timeless evil, an impression of a ghastly malign intelligence. Its stare had been the unrelenting, immobile and utterly emotionless gaze of a serpent or lizard—and of course, the basilisk *was* a lizard. Just a lizard, Garth told himself.

Its stench was strong now; it held all the rot and decay that the catacombs lacked. It was a dry, burning smell, the smell of something long dead, or of death itself. Garth steeled himself and opened his eyes again, trying to avoid meeting the thing's reflected glare.

He looked at it as it stood, unmoving, perhaps twenty feet away. A golden ridge ran the length of its graceful, sleekly powerful body, ending in a crest atop its narrow head in the shape of a seven-pointed coronet. It had a long, narrow jaw, lined with hundreds, perhaps thousands, of small, needle-sharp teeth; a long black tongue flicked silently. Two slit nostrils breathed out a cloud of venom, a pale-silver ghost of vapor in the torchlight. It had four short, sturdy legs with long, clawed toes and, save for its huge size, much the shape of any lesser lizard. Its abominable eyes were unavoidable, though; Garth found his attention being drawn back to them, sucked in by that glittering golden smirk. He tore his gaze away once more, and felt his helmet shift. Fearful lest he should meet its eyes directly, he closed his own and this time kept them shut.

He wondered how old the thing was, and how long it had dwelt beneath Mormoreth; its eyes seemed ageless, as if they had watched the dawn of time with that same unchanging evil. He wondered also what it fed on, here in the empty, lightless, and lifeless crypts, and decided he would rather not know.

He heard a swish; the basilisk was moving. Having more respect for his life than his dignity, he turned and ran helter-skelter down the nearest corridor, only remembering at the last instant that he must not fling aside his stub of a torch; instead, he clutched it tightly as he fled.

When at length he paused, Garth carefully drew forth and lit a fresh torch from the glowing stump he held, licking at his hand where it had been slightly scorched by the flame. That done, he tried to relax, to stop the trembling induced by the sudden burst of adrenalin he had triggered; he breathed deeply and raggedly. If there were gods, he told himself, that creature did indeed serve the god of death, the one whose name was never spoken aloud. He was frightened of the basilisk as he had never before been frightened; its mere gaze induced more fear, more abject terror, than anything else he had ever seen.

He began to think that Shang was right, that the basilisk could not be captured. Further, he admired Shang's courage in entering the crypts to gather its venom, knowing what the basilisk was.

Suddenly he stopped his trembling and admonished himself fiercely that he was panicking, letting fear run away with him as if he were some mere animal, like a rabbit or a human, rather than a thinking, reasoning, and therefore supreme overman. There was nothing that could not be dealt with, he told himself sternly He had to approach the problem objectively. He needed to capture the monster and bring it back alive; that was the basic requirement. He had to entrap it somehow, yet not touch it—as he had been entrapped in the Annamar Pass. Then his only problem would be getting it out past Shang without looking at it.

Clearly, the carved wooden rod he had taken from Dansin was perfect.

He had lost his mirror in his mad dash from the basilisk; it lay somewhere on the stone floor behind him. Fortunately, he had another. He delved into his pack and drew forth both the magic rod and the remaining mirror. He reminded himself to be more careful with these. They were almost all he had left; he had lost his sword, lost the Jewel of Blindness, broken his dagger, and now lost and most likely broken one of his mirrors. Such carelessness was inexcusable.

He had fully regained his nerve. Cautiously, with the mirror held in place with one hand while the other gripped the rod, he advanced back up the corridor, leaving his torch on the floor behind him, so that his shadow lengthened before him as he walked.

The basilisk had moved, apparently in casual pursuit of the fleeing overman. As he approached, it slid out into the corridor, its rich green armor faintly iridescent in the dim torchlight. Garth glimpsed it from the corner of his eye and turned away hurriedly before it looked at him; not caring to risk even the reflected image if he could avoid it, he closed his eyes and began fumbling with the talisman, working by feel.

When he had completed the sequence that was supposed to establish the magical barrier, he cautiously opened his eyes and studied the scene reflected in the mirror. The basilisk was still moving toward him, with a slow and regal pace as befitted the king of lizards. Abruptly it stopped, its advance halted in mid-stride. It hissed angrily, and Garth felt dizzy and ill from the monster's noxious breath. It explored to either side, and still encountered resistance; rearing up, its lighter-colored belly scales flashing in the torchlight, it seemed to climb in thin air, only to slide back awkwardly. It could not climb the barrier, lizard or no.

Apparently that barrier, which could not be budged from the inside, could adjust to outside pressures, since it had narrowed to fit inside the corridor's dimensions.

Garth was satisfied. He turned his back on the basilisk and went to recover his torch. He was extremely pleased with himself; he had captured the creature, fulfilling his quest and defying Shang with the wizard's own device. All that remained was to transport the basilisk safely back to Skelleth. Of course, that might be a bit difficult. He still had to get the thing out of the crypts and beyond the city without encountering Shang. It was a great pity that he had lost the invisibility charm; even with its various disabilities, it could be useful.

He stooped and picked up the torch, then turned far enough to see the basilisk's reflection. He froze. It had come further down the corridor; it was scarcely as far away as it had been when he turned, though he had walked a dozen yards.

To his inexpressible relief, it stopped short, just as it had done before, and at the same distance. He had forgotten that the invisible wall would move as he moved, maintaining a constant distance from the generating talisman.

He caught a glimpse of the monster's eyes in the mirror, and an involuntary shudder ran through him. The calm evil in its gaze had been replaced with hatred, an emotion so intense that even Garth could not mistake it. Its regal air of detachment had vanished; its muscles were tensed with fury. The overman tore his gaze from the mirror and turned to face directly away from the monster again. Carefully, he removed the glass from its perch and wrapped it in a bit of cloth before putting it in his pack. He did not care to look at his catch again, either in reflection or directly; he reluctantly admitted to himself that he was afraid to.

The capture itself accomplished, he now had to get out. Again, he regretted that he had not thought to equip himself with a thread. Instead he would have to find his way out from memory, and without ever looking behind him; this latter necessity was stronger than any bargain or geas, it was a matter of personal survival. Yet as he began to walk he found himself possessed of a growing urge to turn and look, to make sure that his prize was still there, still secure—and no closer. Further, the thing's infernal gaze had a fascination all its own, and it took an effort of will not to seek it out.

It took him several hours to find the stairs leading up to the wine cellar; he repeatedly made wrong turns, only realizing that a corridor was unfamiliar when he had traversed half its length and having to retrace his own steps carefully backward, pressing the basilisk and its magical enclosure back—for the basilisk, though it willingly moved toward him, refused to retreat under its own power and had to be pushed along. This was done by moving the wooden rod that controlled the cage with force sufficient to move the monster, which must have weighed a good two hundred pounds. This dragging, when combined with the poisonous fumes the thing emitted and the corrosive trail its venom left on the stone floors, made any doubling back an ordeal, leaving Garth tired and weak. By the time he finally stumbled upon the steps he was exhausted and sick, his boots worn almost through by the venom-stained floors. He collapsed onto the staircase and rested for several minutes.

Rising at last, he started up the steps, and proceeded without difficulty up the first thirty or forty; then, abruptly, he lost his balance and fell back, as if an invisible hand had grabbed at him and yanked. Only by closing his eyes immediately did he avoid looking back at the basilisk. As he fell, he could hear the monster hissing angrily. Then something caught him, just as something had thrown him off balance, and he realized what it was; the talisman, which he carried in his belt, was responsible. The basilisk had followed willingly as far as the foot of the staircase, then balked. It was when the rear of the invisible cage collided with two hundred pounds of braced basilisk that he had been thrown off balance, and he had been caught again by the rod when the front of the cage encountered the basilisk, which had refused to retreat just as firmly as it had refused to climb the stairs.

It appeared that he would have to drag the creature up the winding staircase step by step. He wished Koros were here to do the hauling, though of course the huge warbeast would not have fit on the narrow stairs. Again he felt weak and sick. But telling himself it was necessary, he clambered to his feet, eyes still closed, and renewed his climb, this time moving slowly and carefully so as not to overbalance again.

As he started upward, he realized that he had lost his current torch; he opened his eyes on complete blackness. He shrugged. It mattered little, since he could scarcely go wrong from this point on. All it meant was that he was safe from the basilisk's gaze. Without thinking, he started to turn for a glance behind him. It was only the superhuman speed of an overman's reactions that stopped him in time when, as his head came around, he caught a sickly greenish glimmer; the basilisk had some luminescence of its own. Unable to resist, he rummaged in his pack and drew forth his remaining mirror; in it he saw that the creature's scales had a dim, silky blue-green phosphorescence, while its golden eyes glowed with an unnatural light that seemed as bright in the stygian gloom as the full moon at midnight. The glow enhanced the hypnotic spell of the monster's gaze. Garth had no idea what happened nor how much time passed from his first glimpse of the eerie illumination to the breaking of the mesmeric spell when the basilisk, unable to pass the protective barrier, gave up and blinked.

Instantly, when that blink came, Garth shut his own eyes and turned again. Then, after a moment for rest and recuperation, he proceeded, managing to drag the monster up onto the first step only by exerting every ounce of his remaining strength. Fortunately, the basilisk itself was unable to move the barrier, no matter how little resistance Garth provided; this was one distinct advantage the magical device had over any more usual net or cage.

Weakened as he was by the poisoned air, Garth found he had to rest several minutes after each step was surmounted. He began to lust after the scent of fresh air as he had never before lusted for anything, save in the sexual fit induced by an overwoman in heat.

To his immense relief, just as he thought he might be unable to reach the wine-cellar before losing consciousness completely and probably permanently, the basilisk gave up its resistance and began to crawl reluctantly upward under its own power. Apparently, now that it was out of sight of the crypts proper, it had decided it preferred cooperation to the tiring and probably painful struggle against the unseen and impenetrable wall that had pushed it so far. It still lingered at the lower end of the cage, but now moved upward at the first touch of the advancing barrier. Garth knew that this was the turning point, that he could make it the rest of the way now.

It was not very much later that he felt in front of himself only to scratch his outstretched hand rather painfully on one of the iron spikes set in the door that divided the crypts from the wine-cellar. Upon close investigation, he noticed that there was a faint trace of light seeping in around the edges of the portal. He paused, but decided against waiting for it to vanish; it was most likely another torch accidentally left burning. Furthermore, even if Shang were just beyond, he doubted he had the stamina to wait for very long in the poisonous air of the crypts. The element of surprise would undoubtedly be on his side if he emerged immediately, and any delay could only weaken him further.

The decision made, he drew his broken dirk and worked it into the crack he had left between the door and its frame. With a slight tug, the portal swung inward. As soon as the opening was wide enough, he sprang through into the wine-cellar, barely able to keep from falling headlong in his debilitated condition.

He was blinded temporarily by the sudden blaze of light after his long sojourn in complete darkness; when his sight returned, he found himself facing a wine-rack as if to impale it upon his blunted dagger. He crouched in a fighting stance and looked about.

The cellar was brightly lit, not merely by comparison with the crypts but in fact; torches flared cheerily in every bracket, though he knew he had left several of them empty. Also, it seemed that there were more empty wine-racks; less than half of those in sight held so much as a single bottle. Something had happened.

Befuddled as he was by exhaustion, the bright light, and enough basilisk venom to kill a dozen men, it was several minutes before he thought to look toward the stairs that led to the palace kitchen. When he did, he saw Shang standing at their head, leaning casually on the iron rail and watching the confused overman with sardonic amusement.

When the wizard saw Garth's gaze turn toward him, he laughed, a long and loud laugh. "Well, overman, you would appear to have survived," he said.

Garth made no answer.

"Are you ready now to concede your task impossible and to depart in peace?"

"Perhaps." Garth's voice was hoarse and unpleasant. He tried to clear his throat, with little success.

"It was rather careless of you to leave your sword cluttering up my kitchen floor, you know."

"Ah." His voice was little more than a croak. "Is that where it was?" It took an effort to make any reply at all, but his own self-respect demanded that he not let this upstart human verbally dominate him.

"I take it that your stay in my little catacomb was less than pleasant. You look quite bedraggled."

Garth did not answer; instead he began to wonder what Shang meant to do.

"It was careless to lose the Jewel of Blindness, too; at least, I assume you lost it. By now, even your slow mind would have remembered it, if you still had it, yet I can still see you."

"You speak, but make no sense."

"Do not pretend ignorance. When I see a broadsword appear from thin air before my eyes, I know that magic is in use. You brought none with you, I'm sure; the Forgotten King would not make free with his own, and everyone knows that overmen use no sorcery. So you must have taken it from that fool bandit I entrusted it to. Undoubtedly he told you how to work it, fearing your sword more than he feared my vengeance."

"Undoubtedly, save that dead men do not often trouble to explain such matters to their slayers."

"Indeed. Well, nonetheless, here you are, and you would appear to be without the Jewel. You also lack your sword, and your dagger appears damaged, which makes it rather useless. This leaves only the axe slung on your back. Would you care to match it against my magic, or will you go peacefully, giving me your word that you will not serve him whom you call the Forgotten King?"

"This axe is not my only weapon."

"No?"

"No. Permit me to show you." He stepped forward, trying to look natural as he struggled to pull the basilisk from the tunnel. To his consternation, the monster hissed in annoyance.

Shang froze. Garth grinned and gave up all pretense, struggling to drag the basilisk out into the cellar.

The wizard closed his eyes and spoke. "I trust, overman, that you have that beast under control."

"I do, wizard."

"I assume that you turned yet another of my devices to your own ends."

"Perhaps."

"You waylaid Dansin, no doubt. I have been over-confident. When next I meet a representative of that yellow-clad demon, I will be more cautious."

"I think it unlikely you will ever meet another."

"It will not concern you in any case. You will recall that I told you I would kill you if you captured the basilisk."

"We all make foolish remarks on occasion." Garth thought that the scrabbling, scratching sounds of the basilisk's progress had changed, indicating that it was past the doorway. He did not care to look to verify the fact. He moved another foot or two, then stopped.

"Before I dispose of you, I must compliment you on your success. I was not sure that the Sealing Rod would hold such a creature."

"It works quite well, thank you."

"Have you any final words, a message for your family, perhaps?"

"I think not; I have no intention of dying." Garth wondered what Shang planned to do; he was rather limited in his actions by the need to keep from meeting the basilisk's gaze. As the overman watched, Shang reached up for the torch beside his head.

"It is a shame that your intentions will not alter the fact."

Some instinct of caution told Garth that even with his eyes shut, Shang could be deadly. He suddenly decided that a retreat would be in order.

Shang held the torch now, having found it by touch. He turned back toward the cellar and spoke three words that Garth could not understand. The words echoed unnaturally, ringing from wall to wall—magic of some kind. Closing his eyes, Garth dove for the door to the crypts, flinging the basilisk, hissing in protest, back down the stairs. He turned and looked again just in time to see Shang fling the torch amidst the wine-racks, where it exploded with a blinding flash and a wave of heat in a burst of supernatural flame that ignited the racks on all sides. They blazed up brightly, and the flames spread rapidly. Struggling with the reluctant lizard, Garth forced his way hurriedly back into the tunnel. Even there the heat was like a blast furnace. From the corner of his eye, Garth could see Shang leaving the cellar, his sleeve shielding his eyes from the painfully bright firelight. It was quite possible that he had not seen Garth flee and believed him to be trapped in the inferno that now filled the cellar. Had the torch struck nearer, or between himself and the door, he would most likely be trapped.

He found it necessary to retreat further down the stairs. This time the basilisk did not resist. It was feeling the heat as well. For his own part, Garth noticed that his breastplate bore a new mark where its finish had scorched and blackened, and that his hair was singed and crumbling. Only his leathery hide had saved him from incineration. A human would probably have died almost instantly. Shang's ignorance of the strengths of overmen might well be his undoing.

Seeing no reason to bake himself any more than necessary, Garth retreated further, stopping only when he reached the point where the basilisk was almost in sight of the bottom. Even here, he felt the heat of the flames; despite the curves in the staircase, the tunnel was lit a vivid orange around him. The flame was not magic merely in its origin, but in its nature, burning far hotter than any natural flame could, given such fuel and such a location. Garth was impressed. He wondered if those three incomprehensible words were the entire spell, or whether Shang had prepared things in advance and the words were merely a trigger. The latter would speak more highly for Shang's foresight, but the former for his magical prowess.

When the fire still burned unabated after perhaps half an hour, Garth relaxed and settled down for a long wait. It occurred to him that he might in fact be trapped permanently, but he thought it highly unlikely. Curiously, he found himself thinking more clearly and breathing more easily than he had before; the fire was apparently absorbing or consuming the basilisk's vapors somehow, while it drew cool, clear air up from the depths.

After due consideration, he decided there was nothing to be done until either the fire burned itself out or it became clear that it wasn't going to. Therefore he ate a little of his dwindling store of provisions, took a sip of water from his half-empty canteen, and went to sleep. His last waking thoughts were worried, though; the basilisk had no food or water. He had no idea whether it needed such things or not; he had seen no trace of them in the crypts. And somewhere above ground, Koros would be getting very hungry. It had been at least a day, probably much longer, since he had left the warbeast.

# CHAPTER EIGHT

Although Garth had no way of keeping track of time, he was sure that at least a day, and possibly as much as three days, passed before the heat subsided sufficiently for him to risk venturing back up to the head of the stairs. His food and water were exhausted, though he had been as sparing of his meager supplies as he could tolerate in his enfeebled and overheated condition. The basilisk, as an occasional glance in the mirror revealed, showed no signs of hunger or fatigue.

He had slept only twice during this period, as his slumbers were haunted by confused dreams in which he saw again the basilisk's unspeakable gaze. On both occasions he awoke trembling, unsure of anything except that he feared those baleful eyes as he had never before feared anything.

The orange glow had died down to invisibility within the first few hours, but when Garth had mounted part way up the stairs he was stopped by the unbearable heat that remained. He retreated, but ventured up again every so often, each time going a few steps further, as the wine-cellar cooled. Finally, on one such attempt he came in sight of the door—or at least where the door should be. The dull red light of the embers beyond showed him that the oaken door had burned, its iron hinges hanging limp, partially melted, from their bolts; the bolts themselves sagged. The wooden doorframe was gone, as if it had never been. The hinge-bolts protruded from bare, blackened stone.

A few attempts later, Garth was able to approach closely enough to see the black lumps of metal that dotted the uppermost steps where the spikes had fallen from the burning door. The spikes had melted into hard little puddles, still hot to the touch and half-buried in fine gray ash. The red glow beyond had waned considerably.

Despite the presence of that glow, Garth decided to risk a dash across the cellar. If Shang had seen him retreat to the crypts, which seemed unlikely, he would not expect an escape attempt so soon. Furthermore, thirst was becoming a real problem.

Looking through the burnt-out doorway, Garth saw, in the hellish light, that the wine-cellar was evenly covered to a depth of almost a foot with fine gray ash and lumps of melted glass. Looking toward the stairs to the kitchen, he saw that the iron rail had melted away and been lost in the ash below. The red glow itself came from beneath the ash, in rows that marked where wine-racks had once stood. It gave the cellar floor the appearance of an immense grill, and lit the stone walls and arched stone ceiling eerily. By staying between the glowing areas, Garth hoped to avoid serious burns. However, he realized that his boots, scorched and shredded by basilisk venom, would give little protection. He removed his scarlet cloak and tore it in half, then used each piece to wrap one of his feet. He rather regretted the necessity of such an action; the cloak had been a gift from one of his wives, and had proven useful in the past.

He considered the basilisk, and decided he had no means of protecting it; he would just have to hope that it could survive the brief roasting. He would be slowed down by its weight, at least until he had gone far enough to force it out into the ash. From that point on it should move quickly enough. The monster had already demonstrated that, though stubborn, it was far from stupid.

When his feet were as well protected as he could manage, he nerved himself, took a deep breath, and set out.

The ash was finer than he had thought; his every

step stirred up a gray cloud. The air was too hot to breathe. His feet were baking, his entire body was baking in his armor; his eyes were dry, the hot air distorted everything, and flakes of ash were blinding him. The basilisk was a two-hundred-pound drag; he could barely move it. A misstep, and his foot touched a live coal. The cloth covering flared up briefly, then died again as ash smothered the flame, though it still felt as if it were on fire.

Finally, when he knew that he could not go much further, he was at the stairs. He clambered up the first three, out of the carpet of hot ash, and leaned against the wall. It, too, was hot; he removed his hand quickly. His burnt foot was agonizing. The first thing he saw when his eyes were clear of cinders was smoke rising from the blackened cloth. A closer investigation showed that the bottom of the wrapping was still on fire, a smouldering line of sparks in an irregular and expanding circle revealing the scorched layer beneath. As quickly as he could manage, Garth untied the binding cords and stripped away the smoking rags; underneath, his boot was also black and smouldering, the sole gone completely. He tore it off, then turned to the other foot. It was better, but not much; that boot, too, had to go, tossed into the hot ash below.

His bare feet were uncomfortable on the hot stone of the steps; he moved further up the staircase. As he did, he heard a violent hissing from the far side of the cellar. Remembering at the last minute not to look, he backed down again. Apparently the basilisk had not yet been forced out of the tunnel.

For the first time since he had trapped the monster, he drew out the wooden rod that controlled the invisible barrier and placed it on the third step from the bottom, sweeping away the thin layer of ash. That freed him to move about, while the basilisk remained confined. When he had scouted out the kitchen, he would return and retrieve the talisman.

Limping, favoring his badly scorched left foot, he climbed the stairs. The door at the top was closed.

It had not burned, however; it was lined with steel, and the heat had apparently been insufficient to melt it this far from the main blaze. It was still too hot to touch. Further, the padlock on the other side was apparently in place.

With a growl of annoyance, Garth unslung his axe; there was little room to swing on the railless steps, but he had no alternative.

It took several swings to break through the steel and the wood beyond, but in the end it was done, though the axe's edge was dulled. Once he had a small opening, it was a matter of a few seconds to shatter the rest of the door to kindling and scrap. Unfortunately, as Garth well knew, the noise would undoubtedly bring Shang.

As the last chunk of door flew from the twisted hinges, Garth observed several things simultaneously: The kitchen was flooded with morning sunlight, a bright, cheerful room much as he remembered it; his sword lay on a nearby table; several mirrors had been set up, so that anything emerging from the wine-cellar was confronted with its own image repeated perhaps a dozen times; Shang stood in an open doorway; and the wizard held a cloudy amber disk in his upraised right hand.

Acting instinctively, Garth flung his axe and dove for his sword. His wounded foot betrayed him, and he fell awkwardly to the floor, halfway beneath the table he had meant to reach, while his axe missed the wizard by several inches. Shang ducked as the axe flew by, a matter of reflex; he had been in no danger. As the weapon fell rattling to the floor, the wizard laughed.

"A poor throw, overman." He raised the disk again.

Although Garth had no idea what the thing was, it was plainly a weapon of some sort; in desperation, he drew and flung his broken dagger, momentarily forgetting its blunted tip. Luck was with him; despite its altered balance, the knife flew truly and struck the disk broadside. Had the disk been solid there would have been no result, but it was thin crystal and shattered spectacularly as the flat of the blade hit. Shang screamed as a yellow cloud of something between liquid and vapor settled seething over his hand. Garth caught the now-familiar odor of the basilisk.

Since Shang was plainly incapacitated for the moment, Garth clambered to his feet, leaning heavily on the table, and snatched up his sword; armed, he faced the wizard again.

Garth had hoped that the poison would kill the wizard, but it had not; instead, Shang clutched a blackened stump where his right hand and forearm had been. He glared at Garth, his eyes glittering. Garth guessed that glitter to be pain and hatred made manifest.

"Overman," Shang said, his voice hoarse with agony, "I had meant your death to be quick and painless, a simple transformation; but now you will die slowly."

Garth saw no point in answering a dead man; he knew that, if he were to live, Shang had to die. He made no reply, but approached the crippled and unarmed wizard with raised sword.

He never reached him. Shang made a curious gesture with his remaining hand, and the overman froze in midstride; his muscles would not respond. Despite his mental struggle, his sword began to descend, his limbs to sag; he drooped forward, then fell numbly to the flagstone floor. There was no sensation at all, no pain, no shock as he hit the stone, only the crash of his armor and the rattle of his dropped sword.

"The Cold Death is slow, overman, but it is not excessively painful. I trust that, should we chance to meet in hell, you will not hold my actions against me. Do not bother to struggle; nothing can break the spell while I live and will it. You will only hasten the end by tiring yourself."

Garth heard these words faintly, as if from a great distance. He was losing touch with the outside world, and even with his own body. The pain in his foot was gone; he could no longer feel the heat of his armor; his vision was dimming.

His sense of time faded with the rest, and he had no idea how long he lay motionless on the kitchen floor, staring at the leg of a table; he knew only that his flesh was growing colder, that he was dying. It did not hurt; Shang had been right about that. Garth would have preferred pain, however, to the gradual cessation of feeling that he was experiencing. He had a profound sense of his impotence in the face of this sorcerous death at first, but then this, too, began to fade. His physical sensations were utterly gone, leaving him adrift in total void, where his memories and emotions were also beginning to fade.

Something happened; the spell was disturbed. His sight flickered briefly back into existence, and with it the strength to turn his head. He did, and saw Shang turning away. Hearing returned, and he could make out Shang's worried muttering and a distant crashing. Something was happening, something that had seriously distracted the enchanter.

Then something huge and black flashed through the open door behind Shang, and abruptly the wizard was gone, lost in a ferocious assault of claws and teeth and fur; his screams were swallowed in the hungry growls of the warbeast that had attacked him. Before Garth's dulled eyes, the huge wizard was torn into pieces and devoured.

Although Garth was too far gone in the depths of the Cold Death to feel any surprise, his first conscious thought was that he might have anticipated such a thing. It had clearly been days since Koros was fed. Shang had left one loose end too many; typically careless human behavior.

Then his thoughts were interrupted by the first twinge as sensation began to return, and for several long minutes he was unaware of anything except pain. The return to life was hideously painful, infinitely more so than the slow approach to death had been. His entire body burned with a sensation akin to the stinging felt when a frostbitten member is thawed too quickly, save that it was everywhere in his flesh, and a thousand times more intense. He imagined that even his bones were aching, and whenever he thought the agony was diminishing it would suddenly return, worse than ever.

It was extremely fortunate that Shang had been so large and so plump; a smaller, more typical human would have been insufficient to satisfy the warbeast's hunger, and Garth was hardly in any condition to resist should his mount decide to devour the overman in addition to its first victim.

When at last the after-effects of the Cold Death had subsided to occasional fits of trembling and a generalized weakness and nausea, Garth opened his eyes to see Koros standing calmly a few feet away, contentedly licking the marrow from a broken thighbone. The light seemed dim. He struggled to his feet and rubbed his eyes; the light *was* dim. The kitchen was lit from the east, and the sun was now well past its zenith, so that the chamber was gray and shadowed. That alone told Garth how long he had lain fighting off Shang's final spell. Judging by the altered light and a glance at the shadows visible through the window, Garth decided that the experience had taken the better part of a day, at least six or seven hours.

Which, he realized, meant that the basilisk had been unattended in the burnt-out, stifling-hot cellar for half a day. He started for the shattered cellar door, then stopped, uncertain; how was he to keep Koros from petrifaction?

He looked at the immense beast, and his uncertainty grew. He was not even sure he dared to approach the animal. However, it was plain that he would have to. Cautiously, he retrieved his sword from where it lay and neared the creature. It turned from its morsel and studied him. He could read nothing in its eyes; its catlike gaze, though it held none of the hypnotic horror of the basilisk's, was equally inscrutable, less interpretable even than human emotions, though Garth assumed the warbeast to be a simple and straightforward creature in its behavior when compared with the twisted motivations of men and women.

It did not growl, which encouraged him. Not wanting to antagonize it, he sheathed his sword; the weapon would have been little use against so powerful an adversary in any case, and it was surely intelligent enough to know a weapon when it saw one.

Something in its manner changed, becoming more familiar and reassuring; it seemed less tense.

He said, "Koros . . . beast . . . " then stopped; it understood only commands, and he did not know what command to give. Finally, he arrived at the obvious. "Come here, beast."

Obediently, the monster stretched itself, a leg at a time, and trotted the pace or two necessary to bring its black-furred muzzle a few inches from Garth's face. It blinked and made a low noise in its throat that the overman knew to be an expression of satisfaction or pleasure.

Greatly reassured, Garth patted the huge head and told it, "We go." He pointed to the door through which it had entered, and Koros promptly turned and led the way. Which was, Garth told himself, just as well, since he had no idea of the best route out of the palace.

Looking monstrous and out of place, like a kitten in a doll-house, the warbeast led its master back through a series of dim rooms, tapestried and ornate chambers, until they emerged blinking into the light of the setting sun, which shone pinkly on the white marble walls and the empty marketplace. Descending the three steps to street level, Garth looked about. There were no signs of life. Silence reigned; not so much as a gust of wind could be heard. Regret brought a sigh to Garth's lips; he had hoped that Shang's death would revive the people of Mormoreth, but it had plainly failed to do so. Perhaps, since it was the basilisk's venom that had powered his magic, the spell could be broken by the slaying of the basilisk, but quite aside from the fact that he had agreed to bring it back alive, he had no idea how to go about killing the monster, nor even if it was possible at all. But then again, perhaps some magicks were permanent, deriving from external energies rather than their wielders' personal force.

It suddenly occurred to him that the wooden rod had better have a source of power other than its creator, or else he had not captured the basilisk but merely brought it up and freed it.

Turning, he ordered Koros, "Wait." He remounted the palace steps and retraced his path to the kitchen. He noticed in the entry hall, as he had not before, the ruined remains of the great golden door that Koros had battered apart in its pursuit of fresh meat; the gems had been scattered about the floor, the beaten gold torn from its frame in broad, twisted segments, the solid oaken frame clawed to splinters, as if an entire army had set out to destroy it rather than a single underfed animal. Garth imagined the fury of the warbeast's attack, and shuddered. How, he wondered, could so much raw strength belong to a single animal? And why did such an animal submit to the control of an overman it could kill with a single blow?

Such questions were worrisome and irrelevant; he forgot them, and limped back to the cellar entrance.

It was curious. The warbeast had not harmed anything in the intervening rooms; not a single chair or table was upset, not a single tapestry or ornament damaged. Yet there was the door, and in the kitchen there was Shang. Or rather, there were a few tattered scraps of his gold-embroidered robe, and a few broken bones, as well as smears and spatters of dried blood. Little more remained. A few slivers of glass and a venom-coated broken dagger marked the spot where the wizard had stood when Garth shattered his crystal device, and an upset table was evidence that Koros had not brought him down instantly, but had had a brief struggle. It was a poor end for a man who had

thought himself powerful. There was not even enough
for any sort of ritual interment; even Shang's skull
had been shattered. The largest fragment remaining
was half a jawbone.

It was, Garth supposed, rather ghastly; he had
heard the term, and it seemed to apply. The scene
had very little emotional impact on him, however, in
its physical detail. He had been confronted with gorier
events in the past, involving his own kind. Rather, it
was the symbolic significance which affected him.
Shang had been a man seeking power and glory who
had achieved a measure of both, apparently; yet he
was now just as dead as any creature that died, and
just as powerless. Garth had little doubt that Shang
would be forgotten in a few years.

That was the fate he had made his bargain to
avoid.

# CHAPTER NINE

Pausing at the cellar doorway, Garth reached in his pack for his mirror. He didn't find it; instead he cut a thumb on a razor-sharp shard of glass. The mirror had been shattered by one of the falls he had taken that morning.

Turning back to the kitchen, he once again observed the array of mirrors Shang had set up; they were, as yet, an unexplained mystery. Perhaps they had been somehow intended as a defense against the basilisk. That seemed unreasonable to Garth; surely, if he could tolerate the reflection of the monster's gaze, such a reflection couldn't bother the basilisk itself. Still, Shang must have had something in mind.

Therefore, Garth collected the mirrors and stacked them face down in a corner, taking the smallest to replace his own shattered glass. This done, he made his way cautiously down the cellar stairs, keeping his eyes fixed on the mirror. He wished that the iron railing were still there; he was decidedly unsteady on his scorched bare feet.

The vast chamber was still unbearably hot, but the red glow had died. Garth found himself in gloom alleviated only by the dim gray light that trickled in through the broken doorway. He had to grope to find the talisman. His hand fell upon it at last, and he picked it up, moving back up a step or two, further from the hot ashes that still covered the bottom treads.

The basilisk hissed in annoyance; it was still alive and still confined. Garth breathed a sigh of relief. He considered leaving the creature where it was while he devised a cover for its magical enclosure, but decided that it would be better to remove it from the heat. He had not seen it, and its hissing sounded as healthy as ever, but he doubted it could be happy where it was.

Thus decided, he began hauling the resisting talisman up the steps, struggling to keep his footing. His progress was slow, and he found it necessary to drop his mirror so that his hands were free to use in steadying himself. He closed his eyes and inched upward, dropping to his hands and knees as his tortured soles protested.

The basilisk hissed again, more loudly; in fact, it kept up a steady racket for several minutes, until he was clambering out into the kitchen once more, when it abruptly ceased. He feared that the creature had succumbed, but dared not look back to see. Instead he proceeded on through the open door to the next room, and was immensely relieved when the resistance on the wooden rod suddenly vanished, indicating that the basilisk was again moving under its own power. Once he had that confirmation of its survival, he put down the talisman and shut the door, so that he would not accidentally meet the monster's gaze.

Now he needed something to cover the invisible cage with, or at the very least to rig an opaque barrier of some sort to keep between the warbeast and the basilisk. A large piece of fabric, or several such pieces sewn together, would be perfect. He looked at the tapestries that hung on every wall, but rejected them; they were heavy, and would add too much weight to Koros' burden. A better supply of fabric was available.

He found his way to the entry hall again, and out into the square. The sun had set, and the long shadows were blending into the gathering twilight. Koros was waiting, obediently. It growled slightly upon seeing its master emerge. Garth heard the sound and recognized it as a growl of hunger rather than greeting; already it had digested much of its most recent victim, and had yet to make up fully for its prolonged fast. It was, Garth decided, warning him.

He approached it, patted its muzzle, and stroked its triangular, catlike ears. It made no sound, but merely flattened its ears back against its broad skull. It was not in a mood properly to appreciate such gestures. Garth removed his hand and told it, "Hunt."

Immediately it pricked up its ears again, turned, and trotted away down the avenue that led to the city gate. It would be a long time before it returned, Garth was certain; there was no game to be found in Mormoreth Valley. It would have to find its way to the mountains, track and kill sufficient wildlife to satisfy its vast appetite, then return. Such an enterprise would give him more than enough time to sew a covering from the canopies and curtains of the market's abandoned merchants' stalls.

It was, he discovered, very pleasant to sit and rest, to get off his mistreated feet. He reposed briefly on the palace steps, watching the crimson sunset fade from the western sky, as he considered what he needed. He was unsure of the exact dimensions of the enclosure, most particularly of its height; it seemed to extend for perhaps twenty feet, and could be assumed to be a hemisphere. Its center was at least ten feet high, as he recalled from the occasion in the Annamar Pass when he had been the one enclosed. He would assume that such was its size. If it were less, the extra fabric could drag, or be trimmed away; if it were more, additional cloth could be sewn on. It would take several of the canopies, most of which were less than ten feet across.

He would need needle and thread, of course, but those could doubtless be found in the chambers formerly occupied by the palace women.

The journey back to Skelleth would need provisions, as well; the thought reminded him that he was ravenously hungry. It had been so long since he last ate that he had grown used to the aching in his belly and come to ignore it—particularly since he had been kept busy by other concerns.

One of which had led him to leave the basilisk in the kitchen. A nuisance, that. Still, upon consideration, he decided that food was his first priority. There was no longer any need for haste.

It proved, upon mirrored investigation, that the basilisk was asleep in a corner. Garth did not disturb it by moving the barrier, but crept in as quietly as he could and ransacked those cabinets not cut off by the invisible enclosure. The selection was somewhat limited, since the wall made perhaps a fourth of the cupboards inaccessible, but the overman found several shelves of wine, a large quantity of salted beef sewn in linen to prevent insects from contaminating it, several baskets of reasonably fresh fruit, and other viands sufficient to provide him with a feast such as he had rarely enjoyed. He lost track of time shortly after he had moved his booty into the next room, shut the kitchen door, and lit several candles. He was aware at one point that he had drunk more wine than was wise, and at another that he was extraordinarily sleepy, but most of the evening was simply a blur. He awoke the next day wrapped comfortably in a thick woolen tapestry depicting several nude women dancing about a fountain, with a pain in his belly, a dry throat, and vague memories of unpleasant dreams full of evil, reptilian eyes. The sun was pouring through the courtyard windows, and a glance at the angle told him that it was almost noon. The candles he had lit had all burned down to puddles of congealed wax.

He started to rise, then abruptly changed his mind; the burns on his feet had developed into an oozing, peeling mass of blisters.

Ruefully considering this, it struck him how little life resembled the tales told of past heroes. In the stories, when a quest had attained its goal and those opposing the hero had been slain, the story was at an end. There was never any mention made of difficulties in getting the object of the quest back home.

Wincing, he managed to struggle to his feet. A nearby table held the remains of the preceding night's banquet, and he scraped together a satisfactory breakfast from the leftovers. After he had eaten, the ache in his belly was less, though still there—undoubtedly the result of gorging himself after a fast, stretching the stomach unmercifully. Half a bottle of some unfamiliar golden wine removed the dryness from his throat. He began to feel somewhat better, despite the mess his feet were in. His head seemed remarkably clear now that he was no longer suffering from exhaustion and the peripheral vapors of the basilisk. He rather dreaded the necessity of opening the kitchen door eventually; the atmosphere in there must be quite unhealthy by now.

Fortunately, it could still be put off. He had not yet made a cover for the invisible cage, and that would take a good bit of time. Reluctantly he rose from his breakfast and, tottering on his blisters, set out in search of a needle and thread strong enough for his purpose.

After an hour's search he located a needle and supply of heavy thread in a back storeroom, apparently intended for the repair of saddles; it seemed perfect. He limped back across the courtyard and out into the market, blinking in the noon sun, and began collecting fallen canopies.

Koros returned from its hunt when the shadows were of a length equal with their sources, the hour of midafternoon. Garth had sewn together a dozen large pieces of fabric into a gaily patterned circle a little over thirty feet across, and was debating with himself as to whether it would be sufficient. Koros' return decided him; he would risk it, and maybe get a start on his journey to Skelleth.

He wondered what the warbeast had found to eat. It seemed well fed, though there was little or none of the usual blood on its mouth. It didn't matter, of course, as long as the animal was satisfied.

It would be necessary to get Koros out of sight of

the market temporarily while the cover was put on the cage. Garth had already decided that it would be impractical to try and cover the enclosure while it was still in the palace, where it would become entangled at every doorway. The barrier seemed to accommodate its width to doorways, but the cover, being ordinary cloth, would not be so cooperative.

He led the warbeast to a convenient alley and instructed it to wait. Then it was a matter of mere minutes to fetch the basilisk out and drape the covering over the enclosure. It fit admirably; the cage proved to be about twenty feet in diameter and ten feet high, as he had guessed, so that the skirts of the cover were easily made to touch ground on all sides but did not drag more than a few inches. They did tend to flap somewhat in the breeze, so Garth took the time to lash the chains he had carried in his pack throughout the entire adventure in place at the bottom edges, gratified to be getting some use from them after having gone to the trouble of dragging them about for so long. The added weight acted to keep the cover exactly in place. Standing back a few paces, Garth admired his handiwork; the basilisk could not be seen, and Koros was safe—and so was he. He could look around without worrying about mirrors and such. All there was to be seen was a large hemispherical tent. The basilisk apparently didn't much like its new habitat; it was hissing angrily in protest. He ignored its complaints. He had only agreed to bring it back alive, not to bring it back happy and contented.

It was a matter of minutes to summon Koros, tuck the wooden talisman securely into the warbeast's harness, and mount, removing at long last the weight on his feet. He had become so used to walking on them that the lessening of that pain resulted in a burst of euphoria, as if he were pleasantly drunk. He felt like singing; unfortunately, he knew no songs, and doubted he could carry a tune if he did. Overmen were notoriously unmusical. Instead he chanted, reciting

an elaborately bloodthirsty historical saga that he
had learned as a child. As Koros strode through the
streets of Mormoreth toward the ruined city gate,
Garth lost himself in chanting the tale of one of his
own ancestors who had single-handedly held a city
in the long-ago Racial Wars between men and overmen, the wars that had driven the outnumbered overmen into the Northern Waste.

He had done it, he told himself between stanzas;
he had captured the basilisk, and was now riding
comfortably with his quarry dragging behind him,
its tentlike covering apparently moving of its own
power as it followed Koros without any visible attach-
ment. He was safe from the wizard Shang; though
he had not truly defeated him, nonetheless the wizard
was dead and no longer a threat. He was well fed, his
wounds were minor and healing. Life seemed very
pleasant.

This happy mood could not last; it was ruined when
he reached the city gates and realized that the basilisk's
carefully prepared enclosure would not fit through
them. Garth broke off his chant in annoyance. It
proved necessary to lead Koros well away along the
curvature of the city walls, then to drag the cloth
covering off and out the gate, then to move the enclosure out and reassemble the whole affair. After the
brief respite, the pain in his feet was worse than ever;
he limped badly as he struggled with the recalcitrant
basilisk and its uncooperative cage. When he was
again mounted and moving, he turned sidesaddle
and did what he could to clean and bandage the ruined soles, which were now oozing blood and pus in
equal and copious amounts. The sun was well down
the western sky, and the shadows did nothing to aid
him. In all, when he at last turned his face forward
once more, he had little inclination to resume his chant.
Instead he began to wonder blackly what the Forgotten King could want with a basilisk.

It seemed quite plain that the old man had known
all along what Garth would encounter. Why else would

he have sent the overman on such an errand? There was no point in wondering *how* he had known that the only living thing in the crypts was a basilisk; he had known, most likely through magic. Further, he had not told Garth. Why? To avoid frightening him into abandoning the bargain? It seemed unlikely that the Forgotten King had so badly misjudged his new servant. No, the old man had wanted Garth to be ill prepared. Two possibilities came of that conclusion: either the King had wanted Garth to fail, to die attempting the almost-impossible task, or he had wanted to provide a severe test of Garth's resourcefulness. Perhaps it was a combination; perhaps the task was intended to end in either success or death. The former would prove Garth to the King, and the latter would remove a nuisance.

But there must be thousands of possible quests that would serve such an end. It would have been much simpler to order him to duel to the death with some formidable antagonist. The King must have some use for the basilisk, then; or maybe he considered Shang to be an enemy. No, in that case he would have sent Garth to kill Shang. He had some use for the basilisk.

What possible use is a basilisk?

It provided an unlimited supply of poison, of course, and could be used to turn people to stone. That was why Shang had wanted it. Could the Forgotten King be planning to do to Skelleth what Shang did to Mormoreth? If so, Garth wanted no part of it. Or perhaps he intended to use the basilisk against someone else; the High King at Kholis, perhaps, or worst of all, against Garth's own people, to finish what the Racial Wars started three hundred years ago.

Whatever the old man had in mind, Garth had little doubt it was something evil; it was hard to imagine how the basilisk could be used for anything that was *not* in essence evil. It was a creature of death. As he had told himself in the crypts, if there were gods, the basilisk served the god of death, the being humans called the Final God. He tried to recall everything he knew of that god; there was very little. There was a myth that any being who spoke the true name of the Death-God would die instantly, unless he had already sold himself to an evil power. Also, the Final God had brothers and sisters. Garth had no idea what the forbidden name might be, nor which of the thousands of gods were kin to Death.

If the basilisk were in truth a creature of the Death-God, then did the Forgotten King serve him as well? If so, Garth thought, he might well come to regret his bargain. He wanted no truck with the forces of evil; they were already far too strong for his liking. If he had to sell his life for the immortality of his name, he might settle for a lesser degree of fame.

He would have to discuss matters more thoroughly with the Forgotten King.

The sun was down before he had covered a third of the distance to the foothills of the Annamar Pass, but Garth ignored the darkness and kept Koros moving, dragging the huge cloth cage down the highway. Even in the darkness it was hard to lose one's way, since the road was bounded on either side by high grass. An occasional glance backward in the gathering gloom showed that the vegetation in the unkept roadway and for a few feet on either side withered and died as the basilisk's cage passed over it, further proof, were any needed, of the virulence of the monster's poison.

It was some time around midnight that Garth reached the spot where he had camped before entering Mormoreth, where he had separated from Elmil. It seemed as good a place as any to spend the remainder of the night, he decided. It took perhaps five minutes to unburden the warbeast and secure the Sealing Rod, and five seconds to fall asleep. His last waking thought was to wonder what use the Forgotten King had in mind for the basilisk.

His sleep was uneasy, troubled once again by dreams in which his eyes met the basilisk's gaze, dreams of feeling once again the numbness of the Cold Death as the monster and the Forgotten King watched him perish. Finally, he awoke, to find Elmil standing over him, propped on a rude crutch, with a sword naked in his hand.

He started to rise, but stopped when the bandit made a threatening motion with his sword. Reluctantly, he lay back.

"Greetings, overman."

Garth said nothing.

"You broke your word. I thought the word of an overman was good."

Astonished, Garth said nothing. His eyes widened slightly, but Elmil, having as little experience with overmen as Garth had with humans, noticed nothing.

"Have you an explanation?"

"I am unaware as to how I broke my word."

"You swore that you would not slay Dansin."

"I did not slay Dansin."

"You swore your beast would not slay Dansin."

Garth started to speak, then halted. He had not foreseen such a possibility. He would have to be more careful when setting Koros free to hunt—assuming he lived long enough to do anything. Choosing his words carefully, he said, "I did not order it to slay Dansin."

"Yet it did so."

"I was not aware of this."

Elmil's voice was controlled and steady. Garth could not tell if the bandit was suppressing fear, or rage, or hatred, or was merely tensing in preparation for the kill. "Your beast devoured Dansin without provocation, though you swore it would not."

"It was hungry."

"So you let it feed on my comrade?"

"I did not know what it ate. I was in Mormoreth. I had been trapped in the crypts beneath the palace for several days, and Koros had not been fed. It killed and ate Shang, but was still hungry. I set it free to hunt. I did not know that it would kill Dansin, nor even that he was in the area. Had I not let it hunt, it might have turned on me."

The point of Elmil's sword moved slightly away from Garth's throat. "Shang is dead?"

"Yes."

"You killed him?"

"Koros killed him."

"What is in that tent?" He nodded toward the magic cage.

"The basilisk."

"Basilisk?"

"The monster I was sent to capture."

"What kind of monster?"

"A very poisonous one. Its gaze will turn one to stone."

Elmil said nothing.

"It was the basilisk that permitted Shang to turn the people of Mormoreth to stone. He collected its venom."

"I don't believe it."

"Then look for yourself."

Elmil managed a feeble grin. "Maybe I do believe you, after all."

"Good. May I get up?"

Elmil hobbled back and permitted Garth to sit up. Remembering the sorry condition of his feet, the overman declined to stand.

"You still broke your word."

"True, though it was unintentional. My apologies, though I realize they can do little to comfort you or Dansin."

"It is the custom among my people to pay for a man's death."

"I have little to give for blood-money." An idea struck him. "Except, that is, for the city of Mormoreth, which I took from Shang. Will you accept the city as weregild?"

It was Elmil's turn to be astonished.

"As you know, the people of Mormoreth are no more and, now that Shang is dead, the city is empty.

It's a good city, though there are a few broken doors and rather a lot of statues."

"It is a farmer's city." The barbarian's tone was uncertain, belying his words of rejection.

"Cannot bandits learn farming? Surely it's a more profitable trade, and it is definitely safer."

Elmil grinned. "Very well, Garth Oath-Breaker, we will accept your payment for Dansin's life."

"Good."

"The sun is well up. Will you be riding soon?"

"I suppose I shall."

"Perhaps I will accompany you as far as the South Road."

"If you wish."

"It will be a great surprise to my tribe to hear that we now own the Valley of Mormoreth."

"You paid heavily for it; eleven of your tribesmen are dead."

"True. Those of us who survive will have to take extra wives to compensate."

Garth was unsure whether this was a joke, a fact to be regretted or a pleasurable circumstance, so he said nothing. Human sexuality was utterly incomprehensible to him.

The conversation ceased, and Garth rose, limping, to saddle Koros.

# CHAPTER TEN

Nine days later Garth halted his warbeast as Skelleth came into sight in the distance. He did not care to ride boldly into the village dragging the basilisk's enclosure. For one thing, he doubted it would fit through the narrow, winding streets. For another, such a spectacle would undoubtedly stir up all manner of gossip, and he doubted very much that the Forgotten King would appreciate that. There was also the possibility that some fool would peer under the cloth cover, which was becoming somewhat bedraggled. It had rained twice on the journey home, a foretaste of the spring rains that were due any day now, and the cloth had stretched and sagged while wet. Mud had spattered all along its lower edge, and the constant friction where the chains dragged on the ground had worn away small patches here and there, though fortunately not enough to provide a view of the interior. In all, the thing looked a mess, though it was still serviceable, and Garth's esthetic pride also contributed somewhat to his disinclination to parade through the streets with such a thing trailing behind him.

Recalling his first entry into Skelleth, he decided that it would not even do to ride Koros; if he wanted to avoid being the cause of a crowd of onlookers, he would have to sneak into town on foot, looking as small and human as he could manage. Therefore he would have to leave Koros and the basilisk somewhere where he could find them again but passers-by would not. He knew Koros would keep anyone who happened along at a distance no matter where he left it,

even right where it was in the middle of the highway.
He wanted not merely to keep the basilisk safe, but to
keep it undetected. Glancing about, he made out a
rather scraggly copse off to his left, and decided it
would provide the best cover of anything on the
muddy, lightly farmed plain surrounding Skelleth.

Ten minutes later he was glad that the cloth had
been muddied, as the mud provided some degree of
camouflage; the weather-beaten little trees of the copse
could hardly hide so large an object by themselves.
Having ordered Koros to guard the spot, he turned
and headed again toward the village, wearing a rough
gray cloak he had pieced together from his bolt of
cloth to hide his armor and weapons, and with rags
tied around his otherwise bare feet to protect them
from pebbles and to hide the coarse black fur that
covered them. Fortunately, his burns had healed almost completely on the trek from Mormoreth.

This arrangement had another advantage, he realized; he would be able to inquire as to why the Forgotten King wanted the basilisk. Should he be planning
some great evil, Garth could withhold his knowledge
of the monster's whereabouts, which he could not have
done had he simply hauled the creature directly into
town.

It was an hour's walk to the East Gate, and Garth
spent the time considering the most tactful way to coax
the Forgotten King into explaining what he wanted
with what was undoubtedly the most deadly creature
in the world. It did little good; his mind did not readily
lend itself to verbal subtlety in such matters.

There was no guard at the gate; there had been
none when he left, either. Garth was not surprised.
There had been very few wars in his lifetime or that
of his father, save for minor squabbles and pirate
raids, and there was nothing in Skelleth worth fighting
for in any case. Such a village, in such a desolate region, had little need for guards. However, when he
had passed the ruins into the part of the town that was
still inhabited, he was surprised to see the streets

empty. It was midafternoon, and he would have expected to find women on their way to market, farmers trading with villagers, and dogs and children playing in the street. Instead the streets were deserted.

But they were not quite silent. Garth could hear, coming from somewhere ahead, the sound of a good-sized crowd. It grew louder as he proceeded, and was apparently coming from the market-square in front of the Baron's mansion. Although it would be possible to reach the King's Inn without crossing the square, Garth's curiosity was aroused; he continued toward the sound. As he neared, when the next corner would bring him in sight of the market, the sound suddenly changed from the muttering of a milling, waiting crowd to an expectant hush. The event, whatever it was, was beginning.

He turned the corner and found himself looking at the backs of a dozen people. The whole village had apparently turned out. As unobtrusively as possible, he joined them, and peered over the heads in front of him.

There was a platform in the center of the square, perhaps six feet off the ground and ten feet wide. Three men were on it, two of them standing and the third kneeling before a block of wood. The kneeling man wore the mail shirt and leather breeches of the town's men-at-arms, and was very young and very pale. He seemed upset about something, though Garth's limited understanding of human emotions and expressions prevented him from recognizing the lad's abject terror. The standing men were very different. One was rather fat, wore a black robe, carried a double-bladed axe that Garth assumed to be ceremonial, as it was not sturdy enough in construction to use in battle, and had a rather blank look to his face, while the other, who was decidedly thin and somewhat shorter than average, wore a gaudy tunic of red and gold and an expression that Garth guessed to be resentment. The latter had his hands clasped behind his back and, Garth noticed, a gold circlet on his head. It was he who spoke.

"By virtue of the hereditary grant given my father by Seremir, third of that name, High King at Kholis of Eramma, and by my accession to my father's lands, properties, and titles as enacted in law upon his death, I, Doran of Skelleth, son of Talenn, am rightful Baron of the village and lands of Skelleth and the Northern Waste. As such I am charged with the keeping of the law, with the protection of my realm and the realm of Eramma under the High King, and with the maintenance and promotion of the public welfare." This speech was recited in a sing-song tone; obviously, it was a ritual to be recited before taking an official action, though Garth had no idea what action was about to take place.

"It has been established that Arner, son of Karlen, has disobeyed my laws and orders given for the good of the state, in that he deserted his assigned post without permission. Therefore, as is my right and duty, I hereby decree that he suffer the punishment I have deemed fitting for such an offense and be put to death." He hesitated, briefly, as if unsure of what he wanted to say next. An angry mutter ran through the crowd. Garth, shocked by the realization that he was watching a public execution, stood utterly motionless. Part of his mind was telling him that he should have known all along. What else could such an axe be for? A headsman's axe did not need to cut armor nor parry weapons, so it could be lighter and more fragile than a battle-axe and still serve its purpose.

The Baron's speech was continuing. "Furthermore, inasmuch as the condemned did flee from lawful imprisonment, it is my right and duty to levy further penalties, which in such a case can only be made manifest in the manner of death. However, I have declined to have the condemned put to torture or death by slow fire, but have instead decreed that his death be swift and painless." The Baron's expression was very curious as he said this. Garth could make no sense of it at all. "Further, as is customary, I grant the condemned the right to speak here before the townspeople, though ordinarily this privilege is not granted to a recaptured fugitive. I am being as merciful as the law allows. In exchange, I hope that the condemned will reveal the names of those who assisted his escape, and that he shall forgive me for his death." These last few words seemed strained, as if the man were making a great effort in speaking them. Garth found himself wondering why the Baron was making such a speech; surely it was more than the law required.

"The condemned may speak," announced the black-robed executioner.

Arner, his expression still panic-stricken, though Garth did not recognize it as such, looked desperately out over the crowd. He licked his lips and tried to speak.

"I . . . I . . . I wish to apologize for whatever wrongs I have done. I beg to live, my lord; but I will not . . . I will not say who aided my escape, for they acted from mercy." The Baron was standing totally motion-less, his face frozen, his jaw clenched. The crowd was utterly silent. Garth began to suspect that they were not happy with Arner's imminent death. But desertion, he knew, was ordinarily punished with death. He was puzzled. Why should Arner be an exception? Or rather, why should the villagers want Arner to be an exception?

Arner was speaking again, more strongly this time; his fear had apparently lessened. "The Baron has asked my forgiveness. I will grant it." The Baron looked surprised, an expression much the same in hu-mans and overmen. Arner was addressing the crowd now, rather than the two men beside him on the plat-form. "It makes no difference in any case, for what can the forgiveness of a single soul avail when our Baron has sold himself to the Dark Gods?" A murmur arose. A suspicion appeared in Garth's mind; was Arner trying to incite a riot, an attempt to free him by the population of the entire town? "The Baron who rules our village is in the service of the Lords of Evil! He has brought madness upon himself and woe upon our village! Does he not kill someone every spring, whether they deserve it or not? It is a sacrifice! Why does our trade lessen, and our people starve? Because the evil gods will it, and the Baron allows it! He will execute me, yet he allows overmen to walk our streets unmolested!"

Arner's speech was suddenly cut short. In response to a gesture from the Baron, the executioner clapped a hand across the prisoner's mouth. Beside him, the lord of Skelleth was visibly trembling.

Bringing himself under control, the Baron announced, "The right of the condemned to speak does not allow him to commit further crimes. I will allow Arner to speak further if he will refrain from seditious slander. Although it is not my place to debate with criminals, I must insist that I am not in league with evil gods, and I will not permit it to be said that I am. Furthermore, it was not *I* who permitted an overman to enter Skelleth unescorted, but Arner himself. Otherwise he would not be here. Arner, you may continue."

Arner ceased struggling, and the executioner removed his hand. The condemned man looked around, across the crowd, and seemed to sag. "I have nothing more to say."

"Then let the sentence be carried out." The Baron turned and left the platform. Garth watched, appalled, as Arner was bent over the block. The axe fell.

The executioner knew his job; there was but a single stroke, and a single gout of blood, and it was done.

The overman, meanwhile, was mulling over the Baron's final remarks. How was he involved in Arner's death? Had the post Arner deserted been at the North Gate? If so, it was bad luck on Arner's part that he had happened along when he did. Still, the man had deserted his post, and such a crime was punished by death among humans.

The crowd was beginning to disperse. Garth paid little attention, but stood where he was, waiting for the square to empty sufficiently to allow him to cross, bent over to hide his height and with his face and armor hidden beneath his makeshift cloak as best he could manage in the shadows.

A man cast him a suspicious glance, then moved on. Another paused and looked at the large figure crouched in the gutter. His eyes were sharper than those of the first man, apparently, for he raised a cry.

"The overman is here! The overman is skulking about our streets again!"

The crowd, which had been quiet, began to mutter as the townspeople turned toward this new attraction.

"Silence, man, or you die." Garth hissed his words through his teeth as his hand fell to his sword hilt.

"What do you want here, monster?" It was someone new who spoke. Already a dozen men had ringed Garth in.

"Why do you pollute our village?"

"Are you a creature of the Baron?"

"Why did you want Arner dead?"

Garth realized he had no chance of dispersing this gathering quietly. He stood straight and flung aside his hood and cloak, making sure his sword and armor were visible.

"I meant no harm. It was no doing of mine that Arner died. I did not know of his existence until today, when I heard the noise here and came to investigate. As for my business in Skelleth, it is my own; it has nothing to do with the Baron nor with any of you. Now, let me pass."

"You're not welcome here, monster."

"Go back where you belong."

A lump of mud was flung from somewhere; it flew past Garth's ear and splattered against a wall. This was a bad sign, the overman knew. Words would not harm him, but once the step was taken from words to action it became very easy for matters to get entirely out of hand.

"I want no trouble. Let me go about my business in peace."

A voice came from several rows back. Most of the crowd were now watching the overman. "I've heard it said that overmen have no gods, but I think that's a lie. You serve the Lords of Dus, don't you?"

"I serve no gods."

A second mudball flew by, missing Garth's shoulder by inches; a third splattered messily against his breastplate. He drew his sword. The front row of hecklers tried to step back but was unable to; the crowd pressed too close.

"If you will not let me pass in peace, I go in war. Would you start again the Racial Wars?" Garth spoke in his most booming and impressive tones.

"You make empty threats. Who are you that your death will start a war? Your life for Arner's!" A rock bounced harmlessly from his armor, and he began to wonder who it was who wished him so ill; the same voice had accused him of evil-worship and, he thought, of wanting Arner dead.

"I am Garth of Ordunin, and mighty among overmen. Who are you that taunts from behind others?"

There was no answer except another rock; this one ricocheted ringingly from his helmet. Another dollop of mud stained his armor, then another.

"If you wish my death, I would know your name, so that your fellows will know who to blame when Skelleth is smoking ruin in vengeance for this harassment."

"Monster, you will not be avenged. There are not enough overmen left to harm Skelleth. Perhaps you are the last of your race. Is that why you have fled your homeland?"

"You know nothing of what you speak. Come and face me." Garth thought he had spotted the speaker, a dour old man wearing dark red. His answer brought nothing but more mudballs, however, this time a veritable shower of them. Reluctantly, he prepared to hack his way to safety. Shielding his eyes with his left arm, he raised his sword.

"I give you a final warning, humans. Let me go, or

many of you will die." There was a movement in the crowd. Garth thought he saw helmets. Had the men-at-arms joined the mob?

"Put up your sword, overman! And you people, go home!" The shout came from a man in a steel helmet. Garth recognized him as the captain of the guard who had confronted him on his first arrival. He did not obey, however; the man was still well back in the crowd, and Garth had no desire to get killed before assistance could reach him.

"Go on, go home!" It was a new voice, and Garth saw that a dozen guards were attempting to break up the mob, pulling people away and sending them off.

"With your permission, Captain, I will retain my sword at ready for the moment. But I will use the flat if it becomes necessary to strike."

"Very well. Come on, you, move along!" Garth could see that the guardsmen were also making use of their swords to swat reluctant villagers. In a moment the crowd had diminished by half, and the guards were gathering in a ring around the overman.

"I thank you for your protection, men."

"Don't thank us yet. The Baron sent us to fetch you when he heard the disturbance."

"Oh."

"I trust you have no objections."

"I am not in a position to object."

"Good. Come on." The captain led the way toward the Baron's mansion. The remnants of the crowd parted reluctantly before the dozen swords that ringed the overman. They had crossed perhaps half the square when a clod of mud struck Garth's helmet.

"Monster!" The crowd had not been cowed for long.

"Stop that!" The captain sounded genuinely angry.

"Herrenmer, don't you care that that monster is responsible for Arner's death?"

"Arner deserted his post, Darsen. The overman didn't kill him." The captain's voice was cold as he answered the red-garbed old man. The taunter wasn't easily stopped, however.

"What about you, Tarl? Why are you protecting the monster?"

"To get my pay, Darsen." That got a laugh from the crowd. Garth was glad that the mood seemed to be lightened somewhat. No more mud flew, and he and his escort reached the elegantly carved door of the mansion without further incident. The captain opened it, and Garth stepped in. The captain and two others followed, while the remainder stayed on guard outside.

The antechamber was pleasant enough, though small; it was hung with woolen tapestries done in very few colors, with no gold or silver, and floor, ceiling, and walls were all of wood. Skelleth was not wealthy enough to have numerous dyes, nor to waste rare metals on ornaments, nor to import marble or other stones. Granite and basalt suitable for building could be found in the hills to the north, however, and Garth was slightly startled that none had been used for the floor.

He had little time to consider such matters; rather more quickly than he had expected, and with a complete lack of ceremony, he was ushered into the Baron's audience chamber. His three-man escort remained with him.

The chamber was perhaps twenty feet wide and twice as long, with an acceptably high ceiling. Once again, tapestry covered the walls, save where three windows, rather above eye level, admitted grayish daylight. A little brief consideration told Garth that those windows faced north, which explained the poor light, and opened onto the alley where the King's Inn lay, which explained why they were so high off the floor. Who wanted a view of that mess?

Below the middle window stood a large, unadorned oaken chair. The Baron, still wearing the elaborately embroidered red and gold he had worn at Arner's execution, sat sprawled sideways thereon.

"Greetings, overman."

Garth was unsure of the proper ceremonial for the occasion, but since the guards were not kneeling or bowing, he decided that any such sign of respect on his part might be construed as obsequiousness. He merely stood as he said, "Greetings, my lord Baron." He was glad he had thought to sheathe his sword in the antechamber. Though he might want to attempt an escape out the windows, the sword would do less good than having both hands free, and could easily have offended the Baron. At the very least it would have put him on guard.

Considering the possibility of escape, he began gauging the distance to the windows with his eye. It would take several steps and a leap, and then he would have to break the glass and frame—naturally, considering the alleyway's odor, the windows were not designed to open. There were only six men in the room: his three guards, the Baron, and two courtiers, probably the only two the town had. Escape would be possible if this audience went badly.

The Baron had been considering him silently.

"Who are you?"

"I am Garth of Ordunin."

"Ordunin being the overmen's city on the northeast coast, I believe."

"That is quite correct."

"What brings you to Skelleth?"

"I was just passing through."

"I find that highly unlikely. Where were you bound, that it was necessary to pass through Skelleth?"

"I passed through before en route to Mormoreth, and was able to obtain provisions here for the journey. I had hoped to do the same for my return to Ordunin."

"What did you want in Mormoreth?"

"I had been sent to find something."

"Oh? Did you?"

"Find it?"

"Yes."

"No."

"How unfortunate. What was it?"

"A gem."

"What gem?"

"We had heard that there was a gem in Mormoreth that could turn an overman invisible."

"Oh? But you couldn't find it?"

"No."

"Who sent you after it?"

"The Wise Women of Ordunin."

"Who are they?"

"Oracles that live near Ordunin."

"Why did they send you for this gem?"

"I should think that would be obvious; such a gem would be extremely valuable."

"Why did they send you, rather than someone else?"

"I am reputed among my people to be fairly competent."

"I see. So you went to Mormoreth seeking this gem. On foot?"

"No."

"Then where is your mount?"

"My warbeast was slain by bandits on the Plain of Derbarok."

"Yet you escaped?"

"I surrendered my gold, and they let me go."

"While you still had your sword?"

"Yes." Garth realized he had made a mistake, but it was too late to correct it.

"Curious."

"I had slain several, and they did not wish to fight further."

"Ah, of course. Bandits are a cowardly lot."

Garth shrugged.

"So you made the journey to Mormoreth and back in four weeks. I take it you encountered the bandits on your return trip?"

"Yes."

"How did you avoid them on the journey thither?"

"Luck."

"Ah. And how long were you in Mormoreth, searching for this gem?"

"I don't recall, exactly."

"Oh."

There was a pause, then the Baron continued, "And now you're passing through again, on the way to Ordunin."

"That's right."

"You are in Skelleth only to obtain provisions."

"Yes."

"It took two days at the King's Inn to gather supplies for the journey to Mormoreth?"

"Yes." Garth did not like the direction the questions were taking.

"And for this quest after a magic jewel, you needed chains, rope, a cage for pigeons though you had none with you, and a bolt of good cloth."

"I hoped to trade for the gem."

"With such worthless items you hoped to buy an enchanted gem? You are an optimist, aren't you?"

Garth shrugged again; he hoped the gesture seemed natural.

"What of your gold?"

"I had little with me."

"Then with what did you buy your freedom from the bandits in Derbarok?"

"What little I had, which I had gotten for my goods in Mormoreth."

"And, poverty-stricken though you were, you spent a good bit of gold here in Skelleth feeding an old man? And I have heard that the stable-boy who tended your warbeast mysteriously acquired enough gold to buy a share in the last ice-caravan, as well. Could that gold have been yours?"

"I . . . " Garth stopped. He could not think of a reasonable answer.

"And how is it that these 'Wise Women' sent you south with little gold? That, my friend, was *not* wise."

"Very well. I did have a great deal of gold. The ropes and chains were to take hostages, should my offer of gold for the gem be refused."

"Ah, that's better. And the cage?"

"I bought no cage."

"The carpenter Findalan says you did."

"He is mistaken."

"That seems unlikely."

Garth shrugged again.

"And what of the old man you spoke with?"

"He seemed congenial, and I needed to learn the route to Mormoreth."

"I see. He must have been very congenial indeed."

Another shrug.

"However, I have heard otherwise from every other person who has spoken with this old man."

"Oh?"

"He is well known in Skelleth as the surliest, most unfriendly creature in Eramma."

"Perhaps he likes overmen."

"Perhaps." The Baron shifted position, so that he was sitting up. He leaned forward to rest his elbows on his knees, and put his hands together, resting his chin on his fingers. "Do you know his name?"

"No."

"You didn't ask?"

"It seemed unimportant."

"I would be interested in learning his name."

"Why?"

"That man has lived in the King's Inn since before I was born, yet no one seems to know his name. He is referred to simply as 'the old man,' which seems lacking in respect. I would like to call him by his right name."

"I am sorry; I did not ask."

"It has been said that the old man is a wizard of some sort."

"I wouldn't know."

"Tell me about Mormoreth. I have never been there."

Garth was caught by surprise by the sudden change of subject. "Well, it's . . . it's a city of white marble, in the middle of a fertile valley—"

"I know all that. What of the Baron of Mormoreth?"

"There is no Baron of Mormoreth. The city is ruled by a wizard named Shang." It did not seem wise to admit that Garth had left the city in the hands of bandits.

"Oh. Did you meet this wizard?"

"No."

"Why not? I should think he would be the obvious owner of this magical gem you sought."

"Perhaps; but he does not allow visitors."

"But surely, a . . . a *person* as resourceful as yourself would not let a mere detail like that stop him!"

"I did not care to start any trouble."

"Oh. Yet you started trouble here."

"Not intentionally. I wished no trouble. Your villagers wished otherwise."

"Ah, yes, I understand they blame you for today's execution."

"Some of them, yes."

"Just as well that they blame you and not me. They liked Arner far too well to blame *him,* but *somebody* must be responsible." The Baron smiled. Garth did not like the expression.

"Tell me, Garth, how did the bandits manage to kill your warbeast?"

"A sword through its eye."

"Do you expect me to believe any of this?"

There was no change in tone or expression, and Garth groped awkwardly for an answer.

"It's true!" was all he could manage.

"Some of it may be."

"Believe what you will, I have spoken the truth." On occasion, Garth added mentally.

"Why did you not obtain ropes and chains in Ordunin?"

"I knew I could get them here, and I did not wish to burden my mount unnecessarily."

"Are you aware it is no further from the port of Lagur to Mormoreth than it is from Ordunin to Skelleth? There are no bandits if one goes by sea."

"There are pirates. And I was not aware that Mormoreth was near Lagur. As I mentioned before, I had to ask the old man for directions."

"The Wise Women did not know?"

"No."

"You have no old maps in Ordunin? Mormoreth is a thousand years old."

"Our maps are untrustworthy."

"Less trustworthy than directions obtained from a senile old fool in a tavern?"

"It seemed so at the time."

"So you went a dozen leagues or more out of your way to visit Skelleth."

"Yes."

"I will tell you, Garth of Ordunin, what I believe of your tale. I believe you went to Mormoreth. That is all; the rest is all lies."

"Believe what you will."

"I do not believe that a bandit in Derbarok killed your warbeast but let you live. When did this take place?"

"Five days ago." That was, in fact, when he had passed the site of his first battle with the bandits.

"You made the journey from Derbarok to Skelleth on foot in five days?"

Garth realized he had made another mistake, and made no answer.

"I understand that, when the crowd was threatening you, you warned them that your fellow overmen would avenge your death."

"I did."

"But what if I send a messenger demanding ransom for you, and hold you prisoner here?"

"By what law?"

"As a trespassing enemy. As you must be aware,

Eramma never concluded peace with your people. We are still nominally at war with all overmen. Why else must all your trade be by sea? Why else have no overmen visited Skelleth in three centuries?"

"Holding me could make the war an actuality again."

"I think that unlikely. Surely a modest ransom is preferable to slaughter."

Garth had no answer. The Baron was quite correct.

"Do you still claim that you return empty-handed from Mormoreth, that your visits to Skelleth are merely for provisions?"

"No. My visits to Skelleth are what I say, but I have lied as to the rest. Should you imprison me, my warbeast will come seeking me and undoubtedly kill a good many of your people before it can be stopped."

"Ah! And where is this beast?"

"I left it in hiding near the city wall."

"And why, pray, did you not ride into town as before?"

"I did not wish to create a disturbance."

"That could be the reason, but I doubt it; no, I think you left the beast to guard something. I think your quest to Mormoreth was successful."

"Why would I leave the beast and the magic gem elsewhere? I could easily hide such a gem on my person. And for that matter, if I had a gem that renders one invisible, would I have been seen, assaulted, and captured?"

"Perhaps you do not know how to use such a gem. However, I prefer to believe that that, too, is a set of lies. You went to Mormoreth for something too large to conceal, if in truth it was Mormoreth you visited. No, I believe that you hold a prisoner. Why else the chains and ropes? Or perhaps some valuable beast, which you keep caged. You came to Skelleth because the old man had made his interest known. You agreed on the price, perhaps, and now return to arrange delivery."

Garth was dumbfounded by how close the Baron's

guess came to the truth. Could the man be a seer of some sort?

"Now, surely, this would make more sense than a futile search for an untrustworthy trinket like an invisible jewel? The only question is the nature of your captive."

"You seem very apt at deluding yourself."

"Oh? I do not think I delude myself. You yourself say that your warbeast waits somewhere nearby. Why not escort me to it, and we will see whether or not it guards some worthy prize?"

"Why should I do that?"

"To purchase your freedom."

"But you cannot hold me for long in any case. Koros will free me or die in the attempt, and I doubt you want that."

"Koros being your warbeast? Well, even should the beast be loyal enough to do as you say, it would be slain before it could reach you in the dungeon. I care little for the villagers it may kill. Skelleth is overcrowded and starving. Further, such an attack would permit me to reverse your earlier threat. The High King at Kholis might welcome an excuse to send his troublesome and warlike barons to a far-off invasion of the Northern Waste. No, Garth, why not avoid all such difficulties and complications? I will make it a wager, of sorts, a bargain you can ill refuse; lead me and an armed escort to your warbeast, and I will let you go free. However, any captives, man or beast, that your mount guards will become my property. Surely that's equitable? If you're telling the truth, you lose nothing at all; if you're lying, you will still be free." The man grinned.

Garth could find no legitimate reason to reject such an offer. It would get the basilisk into Skelleth safely, yet keep it out of the Forgotten King's hands for the moment. Or perhaps it would rid him of the Baron, if he could coax the man into glancing under the covering. And there was a better chance of escape out amid the surrounding farms than here in the Baron's mansion . . . though perhaps escape would be appropriate now. He glanced casually up at the windows again, as if considering the Baron's proposal.

"Oh, by the way, should you escape, we will post a guard at the King's Inn—with crossbows." Garth looked down again, startled and annoyed. Had his thoughts been that obvious? This human apparently had none of the difficulty in interpreting overman expressions that Garth had in reading human ones. He wondered again if the Baron were a seer or wizard. Perhaps he really had sold himself to the gods of evil. That, Garth told himself, was silly; in all likelihood there were no such gods.

"Well, overman, will you lead us to your warbeast?"

"Yes. If I have your oath before these witnesses that you will free me immediately thereafter."

"I will even return your weapons, which I am afraid will have to be confiscated during the journey. To render escape less tempting."

"Very well; your oath."

"How would you have me swear?"

"I know little of human oaths. As you please."

"Very well; I swear by the Seven, by the Seven, and by the One that I will abide by the agreement made and free you if you lead us truly."

As this oath was spoken, Garth watched the face, not of the Baron, but of one of the courtiers listening. The man remained impassive at the first "by the Seven," blanched at the second, and looked confused at "by the One," throwing a quick glance at his lord. Garth guessed that the apparently meaningless numbers did indeed have some theological significance, though he could not imagine what it might be. Pretending comprehension, he nodded. "That will do."

"Good. But it's late. You will be my guest for the night, and we will go in the morning."

# CHAPTER ELEVEN

The next morning Garth awoke at the first light of dawn. He had been given a room in the east end of the mansion, and sunlight seeped through the curtained windows, though the sky was still mostly dark, making patches of gold on the yellow walls.

He was in a comfortable bed and had eaten well as the Baron's dinner guest the night before, but he was not happy. He had had bad dreams again, and furthermore, he did not really like the bargain he had struck with the Baron. He would almost certainly have to hand over the basilisk, and it would be a considerable nuisance recapturing it should the Forgotten King insist he do so.

He rose and dressed. Scarcely had he donned his armor—he had no other garments with him, and the mansion staff had nothing available large enough for his use—when there was a rap at the door. He growled acknowledgement, and the Baron entered, accompanied, as always in Garth's presence, by a pair of guards.

"I see you are up. I trust you slept well?" The Baron appeared slightly irritated, Garth noticed; perhaps his own rest had been uneasy.

"Well enough." Remembering the courtesies due a baron, he added, "Thank you, my lord."

"Then let us be gone."

"As you wish." He watched silently as one of the guards picked up his sword and axe. His broken dagger he had left in Mormoreth, coated with basilisk venom. Although he had no desire to rush matters, he could think of no legitimate reason for delay; he followed as the Baron led the way down the stairs and past the sentries into the town square. There the party paused as a further contingent of half a dozen men-at-arms joined them. Thus reinforced, the Baron bowed infinitesimally and said, "Now, my dear Garth, if you would lead the way." His manner struck the overman as slightly odd, and the sardonic smile that had been present the day before was lacking. Garth wondered what had caused the transformation as he led the way to the East Gate, a drawn sword inches from his back.

Somewhat over an hour later, the entourage arrived at the copse. Koros stood there, waiting placidly. It growled a greeting to its master, while keeping a wary eye on the nine men with him. The party came to a halt a few yards from the cloth-covered enclosure.

The Baron said nothing, but merely looked sourly at the tentlike object. He seemed to sag curiously. When the silence had begun to become oppressive, Herrenmer, the captain of the guard, said, "You made no mention of a camp, overman."

"I had no reason to mention it."

"Your tent is very peculiar. Is such a structure usual for travelers among your people?"

Garth shrugged.

Herrenmer turned to the Baron. "My lord, shall we search the tent?"

The Baron said nothing. Garth interposed, "My lord, can you trust your men? It might be best if you searched for yourself, if I did indeed bring some great treasure from Mormoreth."

The Baron's slight frown turned into a baleful glare. He picked one of his men, one Garth had not seen before that morning, and demanded, "How much money have you got?"

The man looked startled, and pulled out a purse. It held four silver coins.

"You search."

The man selected bowed and said, "Yes, my lord."

Resignedly, Garth watched as the soldier circled the cage looking for a door-flap. He had made it too obvious that there was some sort of trap. Although the Baron had somehow changed his entire manner from loquacious good humor to gloomy silence over-night, he was still no fool.

The man sent to search announced, "There is no opening. Shall I lift the edge and crawl in?"

The Baron shouted, "Of course, idiot!" The man promptly fell to his knees and began to lift the chain-weighted border. Garth tensed himself to make a sudden move, and closed his eyes. To cover his actions, he yawned; but that failed to fool the Baron.

"Wait!" He looked at Garth, who opened his eyes and looked back. "Around the far side." He glanced at the men behind the overman, and Garth felt the tip of a sword at his back.

Herrenmer said, "Overman, if there is some danger within, I suggest you tell us. The agreement made no allowance for traps, and my men would feel little remorse for killing you if one of their comrades is harmed."

The Baron nodded agreement. Herrenmer called for the searcher to wait. "Is there danger, overman?"

"I believe so," Garth admitted reluctantly.

"Explain," Herrenmer demanded.

"This is not exactly a tent, but a cage. It holds the monster I was sent to capture and bring back alive."

"The monster would tear my man to pieces, I suppose? Then why hasn't it torn the tent?"

"The monster will not harm your man with either teeth or claws. It is enclosed in a magical protective circle."

"Then what danger is there?"

"It is said that the monster's gaze can turn one to stone."

Herrenmer looked utterly disbelieving. The Baron interjected, "What kind of monster?"

"It is called a basilisk."

The Baron nodded gloomily. Herrenmer looked from the overman to his master and back again.

"What," he asked loudly, "is a basilisk?"

"A sort of poisonous lizard," Garth explained.

The Baron muttered, "Your bargain."

"The basilisk is yours, if you want it; that was the agreement. When I am properly armed and safely astride my mount, I will tell you how the enclosure can be moved. I will not tell you how it may be removed, as that was not included in the agreement. It was said only that I would give any spoils to you, not that I would show you how to use them." Garth was rather proud of himself for thinking of this loophole. It had occurred to him on the walk out from the village. "If you do not want the basilisk, I will be glad to take it with me and be on my way."

The Baron snorted. "I daresay. How is the cage worked? I said I would free you and arm you, but a dead overman is as free as a live one."

In response to the Baron's words the sword point at Garth's back jabbed slightly. Koros growled warningly.

"If you kill me, not all of you will live to return to Skelleth."

The Baron had apparently said all he cared to say. Wearily, he motioned to Herrenmer, who said, "What about a revision of the original agreement, or rather an addition to it? Your life in exchange for the workings of the protective circle."

"If you kill me, you will not only not know how to use the enclosure, you will be unable to move it, assuming any of you survive Koros' assault. You will have to kill the warbeast to survive, and I doubt any of you can."

"We have a stalemate, then. You have not turned over your captive as agreed. Therefore, we will take you back to Skelleth and kill you there."

"I will tell you how to move it; freeing it would be far too dangerous. Is that not sufficient?" Garth wished he could reach his sword or his axe; the man carrying them stood off to one side, just a little too far to reach in a single lunge. If he were armed, he was sure he and Koros could easily handle eight soldiers and an unarmed baron.

Herrenmer was obviously unsure of how to respond to Garth's answer. He turned to the Baron, who nodded.

Turning back, he said, "Very well, overman. You may live, and we will free you, in exchange for the basilisk, caged as it is. However, henceforth, you or any other overman passing through these lands must pay tribute to the Baron, as is his right to demand."

Garth considered briefly, then nodded. "The cage may be moved by moving a talisman; I left it over there, partially buried." He pointed, and the soldier sent to search the "tent," who had wandered back to the party, went to find the object indicated. A few seconds later he held up the wooden rod.

Herrenmer asked, "How does it work?"

"Move the rod beyond a certain distance and the cage will follow it. It may require some strength to move."

The man holding the talisman tried to rejoin the group, but stumbled and fell awkwardly backward when the rod he clutched suddenly refused to move beyond a certain point. Turning, he hauled on it with his full strength. Slowly, inch by inch, the rod yielded, and as it did the cage followed, the cloth cover flapping loudly. A loud hissing came from within.

One of the guards said, "Vala, what's that sound?"

"The basilisk," Garth answered. After a pause, he added, "I have fulfilled my end of the agreement. Give me my sword."

The man holding his weapons looked questioningly at his captain, who looked at the Baron. The Baron did nothing. He stood motionless, frowning at the basilisk's enclosure. Shrugging, Herrenmer waved for the man to approach. He obeyed promptly, and began to offer the sword to its owner. Herrenmer interrupted,

"Wait. Overman, your word that you will not harm any of us, nor take back the monster."

"I have given my word that my captive would be surrendered."

"It has been; we ask only a reasonable reassurance before returning your weapons."

"You may have my word that I will leave this place in peace."

Herrenmer glanced at the Baron, who was still frowning detachedly. Seeing no indication that he was even conscious of the conversation taking place, Herrenmer said, "That is sufficient." Garth reached out and received his sword; it felt good to hold it once again. Strapping it on, he glanced at the cage as the basilisk hissed again. It was quite probable that he would have to recapture the damnable monster, and that the sword would be necessary to such an endeavour. He did not look forward to it. With the scabbard secure at his waist, he accepted the proffered hilt of his axe, and slung it on his back in its accustomed place. Thus equipped, he crossed to where Koros waited and hauled saddle and pack into place on the warbeast's back. A moment later the straps were secured, and Garth swung up onto the saddle. The men-at-arms had watched these proceedings with casual interest; they made no comment as Garth turned his mount and rode off northward across the muddy farmland.

It appeared, of course, that Garth was taking the fastest route back to his homeland. This was not the case. Once he was sure he was well out of sight, he turned Koros westward, and proceeded around the northern edge of Skelleth. Since he now knew, from Arner's execution, that a guard was maintained on the North Gate, he avoided that entrance to the town, giving it a wide berth, and instead rode on to the West Gate. It seemed unlikely that any guard would be kept there; no one had any reason to expect any traffic from the west. Garth's rather limited knowledge of geography led him to the conclusion that a road leading west from Skelleth could only lead to the Yprian Coast, which he believed to be inhabited only by a few starving barbarians.

It would have taken three or four hours to reach the West Gate on foot, but the warbeast's steady glide, seemingly unhampered by the mud, covered the distance in an hour and a half. It was still well before noon when Garth dismounted and led Koros cautiously up to the crumbling remains of the town wall.

Three hundred years of neglect, decay, and declining population following the loss of Skelleth's original purpose as a military base and her consequent lack of trade had, as Garth had observed when he first arrived, left the outer limits of Skelleth a desolate ring of ruins, inhabited only by thieves, rats, and outcasts —until such vermin starved to death, as large numbers invariably did every winter, leaving room for a new crop each summer. Some public-spirited official, a century past, had had several of the uninhabited houses pulled down, but the industry of the townspeople had extended no further than that; the roofless, tottering ruins were left where they were. Though they provided very little shelter, it was not shelter Garth sought, but cover. When he had passed the West Gate into this no-man's-land, he turned from the street that led into the village and made his way carefully through the rubble-strewn, overgrown maze of avenues and alleys.

It took him perhaps twenty minutes to find what he sought—a cellar, hidden by two walls that still stood shoulder-high on the side toward the main road, which appeared relatively safe and not unduly difficult to climb out of. It took a moment's coaxing to get Koros to leap down into such an uninviting pit, but Garth had decided that it was necessary to hide the beast somewhere; he plainly could not ride boldly into the village, nor did he care to leave Koros outside the walls advertising its master's presence to anyone who passed—such as the Baron's guards, who might well be set to patrolling the area, in case more overmen approached. This basement would serve admirably as a base of operations, and Garth cared very little whether Koros liked it or not.

It would, however, be a good idea to make sure the warbeast was fed. There was no urgency; it had eaten a day and a half ago, leaving at least twenty-four hours before there was cause to worry.

That left him with nothing to do. He did not dare enter Skelleth proper by daylight, but planned on sneaking to the King's Inn under cover of darkness to speak with the Forgotten King. He could make no further plans until he had discussed the situation. That left him rather at loose ends until sunset, still a good seven hours off.

He polished his sword until it shone; with a suitable stone, he sharpened both sword and axe to a razor edge; he took inventory of his supplies; he brushed down the warbeast; he polished his breastplate; he brushed off his makeshift cloak; he cleared half the cellar so that Koros could move about. By sunset he had exhausted his ingenuity. He spent the last half hour before the skies seemed sufficiently dark in watching the clouds drift and thicken. When he did finally clamber out of the ruins, it was with a better knowledge of the ways of clouds and a suspicion that it would be raining by midnight.

# CHAPTER TWELVE

Crouched awkwardly, Garth stood under an overhanging upper story, dripping wet, his slit nostrils filled with the reek of decaying sewage. The smell, as much as his memory of the route, told him that he had at last found the right alleyway. Unfamiliar as he was with Skelleth, and not daring to use the main thoroughfares, he had wound his way cautiously inward from the ruins, only to become quite lost. His prediction had been fulfilled sooner than he had expected. It was pouring rain two hours after sunset, while he was still attempting to convince himself that he was not lost. The attempt had failed; it was pure luck that finally brought him to the malodorous alleyway behind the baronial mansion, and Garth knew it. The rain had proven a blessing in disguise, in that it had driven everyone indoors, making his detection less likely; but it was a mixed blessing at best, as he was cold, wet, and miserable, and the crowd at the King's Inn was staying late rather than walk home in such a storm. He dared not enter until the mob inside thinned out enough to allow him to walk across the room without bumping elbows on every side. He wished once again that he knew how to curse as he wondered how a tavern in such an appalling neighborhood could attract such a large clientele.

From his refuge, Garth could see up the alley to the back of the Baron's mansion. Lights shone in several windows. From snatches of conversation picked up from passers-by, Garth knew that the Baron had made a triumphal procession out of bringing the basilisk into

Skelleth; the cage had been paraded, safely covered, through the streets to the market square, where it had remained, heavily guarded, until sunset, when onlookers had been chased from the area. It had disappeared when they were allowed to return, and no one knew where it had gone, nor what it was, nor where it came from, nor anything else about the mysterious tentlike object. In short, the knowledge available to the public was no more than Garth would expect, and much less than he had feared. It would not do to have it known that a basilisk was around; some fool would be certain to test its legendary powers of petrifaction.

A movement from the direction of the King's Inn caught his attention. He turned and watched motionlessly as half a dozen drunken farmers reeled and staggered through the puddles toward their homes—or where they drunkenly assumed their homes to lie. Garth was doubtful that they would all make it out of the alley, let alone to their various places of residence. Sure enough, one stumbled and fell headlong in a stinking pool of rainwater and sewage. His companions helped him up, and the whole party was soon out of sight.

The overman guessed it to be about midnight. Abandoning his bit of shelter, he made his way slowly, bent and shuffling, toward the inn. A glance through the window confirmed that, though the crowd had thinned, there were still too many people. A closer look showed that the Forgotten King, invisible in his ragged saffron cloak and hood, was seated in his customary place, as if he had not moved since Garth's departure a month before. It also showed that a good many of the patrons were unconscious, which, combined with the fact that the rain showed no sign of lessening, caused Garth to reconsider risking entry. He was still arguing with himself when a movement off to his left caught his eye.

A man was approaching from the far end of the alley. Even at that distance and despite the rain and darkness, Garth could see that he wore a sword and helmet. The Baron must have set the guards to patrolling the streets.

Without further thought, Garth shuffled through the tavern door and stood, dripping wet, just inside. No one paid him any attention at all; they were all too busy with ale, wine, and conversation. Remembering to retain his stooped posture, he shook himself to dry his garments, then began to inch his way through and around the crowd toward the table where, despite the throng, the Forgotten King sat alone. Behind him he heard the door slam shut. He had left it slightly ajar, and assumed one of the patrons, disliking the cool outside air, had closed it. He did not turn to look for fear of showing his face.

A sudden silence descended over the room, and his curiosity got the better of him. He craned about, as he had seen stiff-jointed old men do, and caught a glimpse of the soldier he had seen on the street and sought to avoid. The man was shaking water from his hair, paying no mind to the wet, cloaked figure halfway across the room. Relieved to see that the guard was not pursuing him, Garth proceeded on to the Forgotten King's table and eased himself into an empty chair. Carefully keeping his face shadowed, he peered around the edge of his hood to see what the soldier would do when he had dried himself somewhat.

He did exactly what anyone would expect a man to do in a tavern on a cold, wet night; he shoved his way to where the innkeeper was dispensing spirits and loudly demanded a pint of warm red wine. The fat, harried fellow ignored other importunities to fetch the beverage requested, and gratefully accepted the coin proffered in exchange before returning to his regular customers.

The soldier downed half the wine at a gulp, then turned and seemed to notice the crowd for the first time.

"What are all you scum doing here?" he demanded. "You know the Baron disapproves of such frivolity."

A voice in the crowd called, "He doesn't approve

of his guards drinking, either." That caused a good bit of laughter. The soldier himself grinned broadly.

"As often as not he doesn't approve of anything at all, 'tis true; but then again, he has spells where he's as merry as any, and in his fits he couldn't care less either way. So, as we don't know his mood just now, if you don't say anything, neither will I, and we'll all be the better for it. The gods know a man needs something to warm his belly on a night like this. But there's another man due in fifteen minutes who may not be so agreeable. The Baron thinks the overman will be trying to sneak back here." That called forth a burst of derision and treasonous remarks about Skelleth's lord, and Garth could make out no more conversation.

He turned to the yellow-robed figure across the table and whispered, "Is there somewhere we can speak privately?"

He was unsure whether the cowled head nodded slightly or not, but a moment later the old man rose and turned as if to go. Garth did likewise, only to find himself following as the Forgotten King led the way upstairs. At the head of the stairs a corridor led toward the front of the building, with four doors opening off either side. It was utterly bare and smelled of dust, a dry, ancient smell despite the rain which rattled on the roof above it. There was no ceiling; the naked rafters and planks of the inn's roof were dimly visible some fifteen feet overhead, and the ridgepole ran along the center of the passage.

Behind them, Garth heard the sound of chairs pushed back and departing feet. The soldier's warning had apparently had some effect, and he wondered if it had been necessary to abandon the cheery tavern for this dark musty corridor that somehow reminded him of the crypts beneath Mormoreth.

Heedless of the darkness, the Forgotten King led the way directly to the farthest door and brought an ornate key out from under his tatters. It clicked loudly, and the door swung open, revealing a large, low-ceilinged room with a broad, many-paned window overlooking the street, whence a dim glow trickled in to provide the only illumination. As Garth stepped across the threshold, the old man reached up to an ornate wrought-iron candelabrum, and the huge tallow cylinder that topped it sprang alight, though Garth had seen no splint, spark, or match. The candle cast a dull, smoky light whereby Garth could make out something of the furnishings.

The room was a bedchamber. A velvet-canopied bed stood against the far wall, with elaborate candelabra on either side, both free-standing and on tables. The light was too dim to distinguish colors, but the velvet coverings reminded Garth of dried blood.

A gust of wind slapped rain against the glass, and Garth looked toward the window. Two low chairs, richly upholstered and resembling none he had ever seen before, stood on either side of a low table that glittered oddly, as if it were made of mica-bearing stone.

The old man motioned toward these chairs. Cautiously, Garth settled his weight on one, and found it surprisingly comfortable, though too low to sit straight in. He adjusted himself as best he could and peered through the gloom at the King.

The silence was finally broken when Garth announced, without preamble, "I have returned from Mormoreth."

The Forgotten King did not deign to reply to so obvious a statement, and after a pause Garth went on, "I brought forth that which I found in the crypts, and it is now in Skelleth."

"Indeed?" The dry, hideous voice startled the overman, though he had heard it before. He had forgotten, while traveling just how harsh it was. Likewise, noticing the hands that clutched the arms of the Forgotten King's chair, he saw all over again how old and withered the man was. His fingers were little more than bone bound in a thin layer of wrinkled skin. His face was hidden, as always, and Garth wondered again what his eyes looked like.

"Yes."

"Then deliver it to me, and we may resolve further the terms of our bargain."

"There are matters to be settled first."

"Indeed?"

"I believe you know what it was I found."

The King made no answer.

"I do not believe you would have set me such a task had you not known its nature."

Again there was no reply.

"Therefore, I believe that you have some use for this creature. When we spoke before, you made mention of certain desires of your own, which required things you do not yet possess. This creature is one of those things, is it not?"

"I have a use for the basilisk."

"What use?"

"That is not your concern."

"Perhaps not; still, I would know what it is."

"That was no part of our agreement."

"True. But when we framed our bargain, I had no idea that I was being sent for so venomous a creature."

"Ah. How does that alter the agreement?"

"I want no part of unleashing so potent a force of death as the basilisk. I can see no use or need for such a creature unless you plan to use it as Shang did, to destroy large numbers of people."

"Nonetheless, I have a use for it, and you have agreed to bring it to me as the first part of our bargain."

"As I told you at our first meeting, I am weary of the omnipresence of death and decay. I do not wish to contribute to the spread of death."

The yellow-clad figure stirred slightly. "Garth, do you know what year this is?"

Garth was puzzled by the apparent change of subject. "It is the year three hundred and forty-four of Ordunin."

"Do you know no other reckoning?"

"The men of Lagur call it the Year of the Dolphin, I believe."

"This is the year two hundred and ninety-nine of the Thirteenth Age, the age in which the goddess P'hul is ascendant over all the world."

"I do not see the significance of this."

"P'hul is the goddess of decay, the handmaiden of death, one of the greatest of the Lords of Dus."

"I still fail to see why this is of any concern to me."

"This is the Age of Decay, Garth. There is nothing you nor anyone can do to prevent the continuance of universal decline, so long as P'hul remains dominant."

"Such fatalism is irrelevant. I do not believe in your gods. And even if I cannot prevent death and decay, at the very least I can avoid contributing to it."

"Perhaps. Yet perhaps not. How many deaths have you caused already upon this errand?"

"A dozen men died that I might bring you the monster."

"One, undoubtedly, was Shang, the wizard responsible for the depopulation of Mormoreth. The rest, I take it, were bandits?"

"Yes."

"You mourn the loss of these twelve?"

"Any death is unfortunate."

"Yet you killed them."

"I acted in self-defense."

"Still, you killed them. Can you really avoid contributing to decay and death?"

Garth was silent for a moment, then answered, "I killed in self-defense. You are under no threat so dire that you need the basilisk to defend you."

"So you will not deliver it?"

"Not unless you first satisfy me that you will not use it to slaughter."

"But I can do that without revealing my purpose."

There was another moment of silence, or rather, a moment in which the only sound was the steady patter of rain at the window. The glow of the single candle flickered. Finally, Garth said, "How?"

"I swear, by my heart and all the gods, that I have no intention of using the basilisk's gaze or venom to slay others. That oath satisfied you once."

Garth said nothing, considering.

"If that is not sufficient, then I will swear further by the God Whose Name Is Not Spoken."

Garth hesitantly said, "I have been warned that you are an evil being."

"Ah. Shang thus warned you?"

"Yes."

"What is evil? Perhaps I merely opposed Shang, who destroyed an innocent city. In any case, even evil beings are not lightly foresworn, and you have heard my oath."

Garth made no answer. He felt slightly ashamed, though he was unsure why.

"Will you fetch now the basilisk?"

Garth cleared his throat. "Yes."

"Good. Deliver it to the stable here at the inn. I will have a place readied."

"There are still things I wish to know," Garth said hesitantly.

"Indeed?"

"I have heard that you have lived here for decades, yet no one knows your name."

"This is true."

"Why?"

"That is not your concern."

"Are you in truth evil, as Shang alleged?"

There was a pause before the old man replied, "I do not know what evil is."

"What is your name, that you have told no one?"

"I was once called Yhtill, a name which surely means nothing to you."

It was indeed meaningless to the overman.

"You have sworn not to misuse the basilisk." Garth was still confused, seeking further reassurance. The Forgotten King's answer was little comfort.

"I am certainly less likely to do harm with it than the Baron of Skelleth, to whom you gave it."

Garth started, wondering how he had known that, then told himself angrily that the old man had undoubtedly heard about the mysterious tent in the market-square and put three and three together when Garth said that the basilisk was in Skelleth. In any case, the remark was undoubtedly true. The overman rose awkwardly from the too-low chair, wrapping his wet, tattered gray cloak about him, and announced, "I will bring it."

The old man said nothing, but merely rose, with an ease and silence surprising in one so aged.

Garth turned to go, then paused. It had occurred to him that there might be soldiers in the tavern, and he did not care to venture boldly past them. Also, he had been away from Koros longer than he had planned, due to losing his way in the rain and winding streets, and, ever insecure, he wished to be sure the warbeast was fed and reasonably comfortable.

He stood, feeling awkward, a few feet from the door.

"You hesitate," the Forgotten King said.

"Yes. I would know if there is a back way. I do not care to go through the tavern again. Your townspeople dislike me, and the guardsmen serve a Baron who has banned overmen from the village."

"Ah."

"Also, I would attend to my warbeast before undertaking the recapture of the basilisk."

"As you wish. I have waited this long; such a delay can mean little. Unfortunately, there is no exit from this place save through the common room. Perhaps you would care to wait while I secure a goat to feed the beast and make sure your route is clear."

"I would be most grateful." Garth might have continued with a remark on how much he appreciated consideration from one he agreed to serve, but he no longer had an audience; the old man—whose unpronounceable name Garth could not bring himself to use—had already left. The overman called after him, hoping he would be heard only by the right ears, "Could you make it two goats?"

There was no answer; silence descended upon the dim room, save for the steady drumming of the rain.

# CHAPTER THIRTEEN

Garth's wait was not long; perhaps fifteen minutes had elapsed when the Forgotten King appeared in the doorway, motioning for the overman to follow. He obeyed promptly, springing up from the chair he had waited in. In truth, he was glad to leave the room, which in its dusty dimness had an atmosphere that unsettled him. During his wait he had studied the furnishings more closely, and noticed that they were stranger than he had at first thought. Beneath a universal layer of dust, the woods and upholsteries could be seen and felt not to be any common substance that the overman was familiar with, but rather unnaturally smooth and somehow alien. What he had at first taken for walnut and ebony had grains unlike any wood Garth knew. What he had taken for leather and velvet had a strange wrongness of texture, and he was certain that no ordinary animal had produced these substances. The whole room was somehow unnatural, as if it were a sorcerous illusion, and he was relieved to be out of it and in the bare but reassuringly normal corridor.

The Forgotten King led the way to the head of the stair, then turned and rasped, "The way is clear. The inn is closed, and the two goats are tied by the stable door."

Garth nodded. "Thank you." he said, as he groped at his belt for his purse. "How much did the goats cost?"

"They are paid for."

Garth paused, and looked closely at the old man.

Almost immediately he regretted doing so, as the man's mummylike hands and hidden face rather unsettled his nerves. He shrugged and left his money where it was. No doubt the King had more than enough gold to pay for such things, even if he hadn't seen fit to use it when last Garth was in Skelleth.

"I thank you again," he said.

"You pamper that animal," the old man replied.

"Better to pamper it than risk letting it become uncontrollably hungry."

"Perhaps." Without further ado Garth turned and strode down the stairs. As the Forgotten King had promised, the common room was empty and dark. The brass fittings of the liquor casks gleamed dully in the dim light that trickled in through the spotless windows, a light that did little to alleviate the blackness. Carefully, Garth crossed the tavern, managing to reach the door with only a single bumped shin. As quietly as he could contrive he slipped the latch, opened the door, and slid through into the noisome damp of the alleyway. There was a narrow overhang above him, so that the rain, which had lightened to a steady drizzle, did not immediately reach him. With that momentary respite, he straightened his cloak, pushed his sword out of sight, and stooped, so that when he stepped from the threshold he seemed once more a bent old man, albeit an exceptionally tall one, with hood pulled well forward to keep the rain from his eyes.

A few paces to his left was the stable door. He headed that way, only to step ankle-deep in a foul-smelling puddle that he had not seen in the dark. The cold water thoroughly soaked the rags he had bound on in lieu of boots, and he wished again he knew some appropriate curse for such occasions. He started to step back out of the water, then changed his mind and strode on; what more could happen?

He promptly cut his newly healed left foot on some sharp object under the even black surface of the water. Growling angrily, he marched on, and emerged without further hurt on the stable threshold. Peering inside, he could see nothing at all, but his hand on the doorframe encountered a tether. He pulled at it, and was answered with the bleating of a goat.

Now it merely remained to get the goats to Koros, then to find and retrieve the basilisk. Dragging the reluctant goats, he marched off westward.

It was well after midnight, and the streets were, as far as the overman could see, utterly deserted. He maintained his stoop and the concealment of his hood, which in any case kept off some of the rain, but decided against struggling through the murky sidestreets, risking losing himself again. He had just concluded that even the high road west from the village square would be safe, and clearly the best and fastest route, as he passed the dark doorway of the King's Inn, when someone stepped from the middle alley of the three that met the one he was in, scarcely a dozen yards away. The dim glow from the few remaining illuminated windows glinted yellowly from his shoulder, and Garth realized the man wore mail—it was one of the Baron's men-at-arms.

It was only common sense, after all, for the Baron to post a guard on the inn. Garth silently reprimanded himself for not expecting it. It was too late to hide; the soldier had seen him. He kept on walking, dragging the goats, as if the man's presence were of no importance to him.

"Ho, there!"

Garth stopped short. He paused a second before replying, glancing about as if to be certain he was the one addressed.

"Yes?" He pitched his voice an octave above its natural range.

"What are you doing here?"

"I'm going home."

"Where's that?"

"West of town."

"Where did you get those goats?"

"Bought them."

"At midnight?"

"This afternoon. I stopped for a drink or two, that's all."

"Well, old man, I know they're stolen as well as you do. But I have orders to stay here and guard this pesthole of an inn. Maybe I could forget I saw you." As the conversation had proceeded both parties had kept moving, so that they were now only a few feet apart from one another, Garth keeping his head low so that all he could see of the soldier was his feet. He didn't see the guard's outstretched palm, but he caught the meaning of his remarks. The man wanted a bribe.

"I have no money, sir, else I'd pay you for your kindness." He tried to make his voice shake as he said that, but the attempt sounded unnatural at best.

The soldier peered at the bent, cloaked figure that still stood as tall as himself, and decided that he wasn't going to get any money without a fight. Annoyed, he ordered, "Well, be off with you, you and your damned goats. And take the rain with you." He turned, disgruntled, and splashed off to his lurking-place in the middle alley.

Trying to sound like any fawning peasant, Garth said, "Yes, sir, and thank you, thank you very much, and bless you, and may the gods keep you safe." He sloshed onward through the puddles, dragging his reluctant goats but being careful not to display too plainly his superhuman strength. It was only when he was well past the center alley, in fact at the corner of the westernmost alley near where he had waited before entering the tavern, that he dared to halt and abandon his role of an elderly human. Growling, he peered through the rain but could see nothing. He doubted that the small, pale eyes of humans were as good as his own blood-red ones, and therefore concluded that if he could see no one, no one could see him. He stood straight long enough to ease a little of the ache in his mistreated back, gave a jerk that sent the goats tumbling and bleating, then resumed his crouch more to keep his face dry than to maintain his façade and marched off through the black and dripping streets.

He made the rest of his journey without incident, looping through the noisome side streets until at last he emerged onto the west road, then making excellent time on that relatively wide, straight and well-drained street. The goats gave up fighting his superior strength, and in fact hurried on willingly, apparently hoping that the overman would get them in out of the rain.

Even though there were no further delays other than the poor footing and visibility caused by the rain, Garth knew that only three hours remained before dawn when he finally found himself looking at the distinctive ruined wall that surrounded his chosen cellar. Since he hoped to slip into the baronial mansion before sunrise, he was hurried and impatient. He called out for Koros while still a dozen yards away.

There was no response.

Oh, well, Garth told himself, the beast must be asleep. He trudged on, leading the goats, which were beginning to show some signs of reluctance. Perhaps they had caught the scent of warbeast.

Splashing through a puddle, Garth rounded a broken wall and peered into the darkness of the basement where he had left Koros. He was unable to distinguish a thing. Here he had no scattered light from the village windows, and the moon and stars were hidden by the clouds. The only light was a dim luminescence that seemed to come from the clouds themselves.

It was hardly surprising that he could not see a black animal, no matter how large, in a pitch-dark hole. He wished he had some means of making a light, but there was nothing around not far too wet to catch a spark from his flint. He called again, to be answered only by the very faintest of echoes. As he continued to look downward, away from the pale glimmer of the sky, he had the impression that his eyes were adjusting to this more absolute darkness, yet the cellar continued to appear a smooth black. It seemed somehow unnatural; suddenly apprehensive, Garth groped for a chip of rubble and tossed it into the cellar, listening for the click of the pebble on the stone floor he had cleared that afternoon.

Instead, he heard a small "ploosh" as the shard struck smooth water, and he realized why he had been apprehensive. His senses, either sight or sound, had detected the fall of rain on water rather than pavement, though he had not immediately realized it. Though the storm had trailed off to little more than a drizzling mist, it was still there. However, Koros wasn't.

The warbeast was more tolerant of water than its feline ancestors, and fully as obedient as one could reasonably expect, but it would scarcely stay in a hole flooded well over a foot deep. Garth crouched, thoughtfully, as he tried to guess where the creature would have gone upon deciding to abandon the place it had been ordered to stay.

It seemed to him that it would do one of four things: it would seek out its master for further instructions; it would go hunting, as it had not been fed for a day or two; it would go home, either to Ordunin or, if its memory was long enough, to Kirpa; or it would merely seek shelter, a dry place where it could wait out the storm. And in any of those four cases, it might eventually return to await Garth.

If it had gone seeking Garth, it might even now be lost in the village, wandering the empty streets in search of him. That could be very bad, but there was nothing Garth could do about it. If it had gone home, well, it was gone. Likewise, if it was hunting, it would come back in its own time and not before, and there was no way Garth could find it. He might search the area on the chance that it merely sought shelter and found some nearby, but the overman did not feel that it would be wise to waste the time. Instead he would leave the goats here, and hurry back to Skelleth after the basilisk. When he had delivered the monster to the Forgotten King there would be time enough to find Koros. The only thing he regretted was that he had left his supplies in the cellar, where they undoubtedly remained somewhere under the dark rain-water. He did not care to venture down there after them.

His decision reached, he looped the goats' tether around a narrow stone that protruded from the ruin and hurried back toward the high road. Without the goats to impede him he made much better time. Though the rain continued, the thin trickle made little difference. He still had better than two hours until dawn when he reached the empty village square.

It bothered him somewhat that Koros had vanished, and also that he had no supplies except his sword and axe, both hidden under his gray patchwork cloak. His feet were both chilled through and thoroughly uncomfortable in their sopping rags, and the cut on his left sole, which had seemed insignificant at first, was becoming painful enough that he found himself limping. He wished that he had found himself a cob-bler and gotten new boots before undertaking any fur-ther adventures. It was too late to turn back now. Koros might be found by the Baron's men at any time, revealing its master's continued presence in Skelleth. Also, the longer the Baron retained the basilisk the more likely harm would be done.

The square was deserted, but the Baron's mansion plainly wasn't. There were lights visible in several of its windows. Still, Garth doubted that there were many people within awake enough to oppose him; most likely the Baron and a few chosen men were doing something, perhaps studying the basilisk.

Though there were lit windows, there were fully as many that were dark. Garth chose a convenient one of these and carefully pried open the casement. The lock gave little resistance, and Garth decided it must not have been properly set. His choice of window had been lucky, he told himself. Then the hinges squealed, and he realized why the lock hadn't held; the case-ment didn't fit its frame correctly, which both loosened the lock and twisted the hinges. He froze momentarily, but there was no sign of activity in response to the sound.

More cautiously than before, he inched the window open a little further until the could squeeze himself through. Slowly he slid himself past the frame, easing his battered feet onto the floor inside gently, lest the floor squeak as the window had.

The room he found himself in was at least as dark as the square outside; darker, in truth, since there was no glow from the illuminated windows here. He could make out no detail at all, though he had a vague idea of the chamber's size. It was medium large, perhaps twenty feet square, with a ceiling that seemed uncomfortably low to the seven-foot overman. There was no sign of life. Garth thought he could see a large dark table in the center of the room, and there was a dim glow under one door as if a torch were lit, not in the next chamber, but in the one beyond. That was the only door he could see in the darkness; others, if there were others, blended invisibly with the walls.

His bare toes, protruding from their wrappings, felt the edge of a lush carpet. Almost without thinking, he reached down, tore off the drenched tatters, and let his bare feet enjoy the feel of the thick, soft pile. He stripped away his dripping cloak as well. He wanted to leave no watery trail through the mansion. Gathering up the wet cloth, he dumped it all unceremoniously out the window, then drew the casement shut, being careful not to let it squeak as it had when opened. He could retrieve the garments in case he wanted to disguise himself again for a leisurely departure, but he would not be encumbered if fast action were necessary. Nor would the wet rags prove that he had entered the mansion, since they were outside. The only evidence inside was the damp spot at the edge of the carpet, which, with luck, would dry out before it was noticed. It had certainly been a considerably neater entrance than that he had contrived in Mormoreth; there was no fallen canopy nor dangling rope this time.

He considered his next move. He had no idea where to find the basilisk. The house was not over-large. It could be searched in less than an hour, ordinarily; the necessity of stealth would not more than double that. He would begin, optimistically, by exploring those rooms he could reach which were unlit and presumably unoccupied.

Feeling his way along the wall, he stumbled slightly against a chair and caught himself with his hand on what felt very much like a doorframe rather than an ordinary wall panel. Detouring around the chair, he inevstigated further and found the latch-handle. It opened readily, and he entered the next room, as dark as the first.

There was no evidence of what he sought; most especially, he could detect no scent of the monster. He groped onward, through another door that admitted him to the entry hall he had seen when first escorted into the house; he could recognize it, even in the dark, by its dimensions, its relative location and its odor of polished wood. The door to the audience chamber was closed, and a bright line of light showed over the top. Interestingly, the bottom met its sill so closely that the overman could not detect as much as a flicker from beneath the heavy doors, but the glow at the top was more than enough to keep him away. Instead he crossed to the far side, where another dark doorway led to the east wing, where he had spent the preceding night.

His nostrils caught a faint whiff of basilisk, and he decided that, wherever it was now, the monster must have been brought in this way. Pausing, he tried to locate the faint scent more exactly, but could not. With a shrug, he crept on through the east doorway. The door itself was wide open.

He was in a hallway. Ahead on his left was the stairway leading to the bedrooms, while ahead on his right a paneled gallery led to the room where he had dined as the Baron's guest. He recalled that there was a door leading under the stairs just before the entrance to the dining hall. It had been closed when he had passed it before.

Peering into the gloom at the head of the stairs he thought he could detect light, and possibly voices. Furthermore, it seemed very unlikely that the Baron would haul the creature up there. He decided to leave any searching of the upper floor for last, and proceeded cautiously down the right-hand gallery. The entrance to the refectory was dark; the door under the stairs wasn't quite. A very faint glimmer could be seen under it, as of a light around at least one corner.

Although the dining hall seemed almost as unlikely as the bedrooms, for the sake of thoroughness Garth decided to investigate it, rather than the illuminated and therefore dangerous doorway. He reached for the latch-handle, only to find it locked. His immediate reaction was to consider this evidence that the basilisk was indeed within; but, recalling his several similar premature guesses in Mormoreth, he paused to consider the matter further. He had the advantage this time of having seen the room, a large and richly furnished chamber. It occurred to him that those furnishings, which included gold candlesticks, were worthy of protection. The door was undoubtedly locked to prevent light-fingered servants from making off with what were probably the most valuable items in the house.

Not that that meant that the basilisk *wasn't* there; it would make sense to put it in a place that had good, solid locks. However, it did mean that, for the moment at least, Garth wouldn't seek it there. He knew almost nothing about picking locks, and forcing them, which he was rather better at, was often a noisy, messy job, and always left traces. Should he not find the monster elsewhere he could always return.

Turning from the locked door he was confronted with the need for decision; he could ignore the faint light and try the door under the stairs, he could move on to the upper floor, or he could retrace his steps to the west wing and check for other doors in the first two rooms he had explored. He sniffed the air, hoping it would yield a clue.

There was a trace of basilisk odor, as there had been in the entrance hall. The basilisk had been brought into the east wing, though once again, he could not tell exactly where.

With a shrug, he turned to the door beneath the stairs; it was closest. It opened readily, admitting the overman to a tiny roomlet, scarcely bigger than a closet, with doors on three of its four sides. He had entered by one of these. Both the others showed light at the bottom, though one was bright and the other dim. The dim one was on his left, and could only lead to stairs going down, parallel to the stairs that ended somewhere over his head. After a brief consideration, Garth was sure that the other led into the kitchens; the door through which the servants had entered during his meal as the Baron's guest was only a few feet away, and it would be logical for the kitchens to be convenient to both dining hall and cellars. It would also be logical to put the basilisk in the cellars, where there would be no need to shutter windows to prevent casual passers-by from glancing in and being petrified. The light under that door was quite faint. Garth decided to risk the stairs. The door opened easily, though with a faint squeak, as if it were not used often.

The stairs were crude blocks of stone descending between rough stone walls. At their foot Garth could see a rectangle of dimly lit whitewashed stone wall and a few feet of flagstone flooring, apparently forming a sort of T with the stairs.

For once Garth was grateful for his bare feet, which permitted him to move silently as he crept down the stairs. He had almost reached the bottom—in fact his foot had just touched the last step—when he heard the rattle of a latch and a door opening, somewhere to his right. He froze. The door closed again. He relaxed slightly, letting out his held breath, then tensed again. There were footsteps approaching, moving at a brisk pace, with no attempt at stealth. Too heavy for the Baron or either of the courtiers Garth had seen, they were undoubtedly those of a guardsman. Silently,

Garth's hand fell to his sword hilt. The steps were very near now, and he heard the clink of chain mail. He drew the sword from its sheath.

The steps halted abruptly, and Garth realized that the man must have heard the hiss of steel against leather. He flattened himself against the right-hand wall, sword held ready. A moment of silence, then the steps began again; this time they advanced slowly and cautiously. At the fourth step Garth judged that his unknown visitor must be well within reach of his sword. At the fifth he tensed, and at the sixth he sprang out to confront the newcomer.

Unfortunately, he had misjudged the distances. He collided awkwardly with the guardsman, and his injured left foot gave way and folded under, so that both of them fell sprawling on the floor with a loud clatter of arms and armor.

Garth was first to recover, and within seconds he was standing over the man, who had not yet risen beyond all fours, with his broadsword at the man's throat. The soldier's own sword lay a yard from his hand, where he had dropped it when he fell. Neither moved for a long moment. Garth was unsure what to do next, while his captive did not dare do anything for fear the overman would slaughter him. Garth studied the situation, keeping his sword where it was.

They stood in a narrow, whitewashed corridor, lit by a pair of torches clamped to the wall a few yards along in the direction the man had come from. Just past the torches, the corridor ended in a heavy wooden door; another, similar door was midway along the right-hand wall. Both were tightly shut. In the opposite direction the corridor opened into a storeroom, its walls lined with wooden casks, which extended back along the wall beside the staircase. It was unlit.

It seemed to Garth that interrogation was in order; he was deciding upon the phrasing of his first question when, with a loud rattle, the door at the end of the corridor swung open.

# CHAPTER FOURTEEN

The newcomer was, of course, another man-at-arms.
He took one look at the scene before him and shouted,
"The overman!" before slamming the door.

Wasting no time, Garth started his questioning and
demanded, "Where is the basilisk?"

His captive promptly pointed to the door that had
just slammed, and answered, "In the dungeon."

"How many men are there?"

"Uh . . . about ten, I guess."

"And the Baron?"

Garth could scarcely hear the affirmative reply because, with much foot-stomping and sword-rattling, the
door was again flung wide, to reveal half a dozen
men-at-arms.

"Surrender, overman!"

Garth merely glared at the soldiers and twitched
his sword so that its tip flashed in the torchlight, less
than an inch from his captive's throat. The man who
had demanded his surrender fell silent, and for a moment no one moved. Then the guards were rudely
shouldered aside, and the Baron strode a pace or two
into the corridor.

"Surrender, overman," he said.

Garth said, "And if I do not?"

The Baron merely nodded toward his men's drawn
swords.

"If I am attacked, this man dies."

The Baron shrugged. "What of it?"

Garth hesitated; he had not expected such open
indifference. "I doubt your handful of farmers can take
me," he said at last.

"If they cannot, I have others."

"You misunderstand. Should you set your men on me, I would consider your death a matter of self-defense."

The Baron considered this, frowning.

"I have come to retrieve the basilisk. Let me take it and I will go in peace."

"No."

"Why not? What use have you for the monster?" Garth was trying his best to be reasonable.

The Baron studied him contemplatively for a long moment, then said, "Why should I tell you?"

"To prevent bloodshed. Perhaps we can reach a compromise."

The Baron said nothing; the silence grew. Garth shifted uneasily, unsure what to do next. His decision was made suddenly when he heard movement above and to his right. There were more guards at the top of the stairs, sent around by another route while the Baron delayed the overman. Enraged at himself for allowing such a ruse, he kicked his captive so that the man rolled awkwardly onto his back. Garth fell back against the corridor wall, his sword ready to meet an onslaught while his left hand freed the axe slung on his back. The stairway door opened and a handful of men burst through, rushing down the first few steps only to freeze when they found the overman alert and ready.

Garth placed a furry foot on the chest of his prisoner to prevent the loss of what little bargaining power the man might provide, then repeated, loudly, his earlier question. "What use do you have for the monster?"

The Baron took his time, studying the overman's face, before replying. "War."

"War against whom? My people?"

"I had not yet decided."

"I do not understand. If you have no enemy, why do you want the basilisk?"

"Let me tell you a little family history, Garth. My

father, damn him, was the commander of the armies of the High King at Kholis; he served long and well, and when he retired from active duty, the king offered him a barony; he was permitted to choose any barony, anywhere in Eramma, that was not currently held.

"Eramma is a large country, overman, the largest in the world; there were a dozen empty thrones available, from Sland to Skelleth. My father, may P'hul devour his soul, chose Skelleth. He had had his fill of court politics and petty border disputes, and so chose a barony so poor, so unpleasant, that no one would ever bother him with such matters. Little did he care what his son might think of ruling such a frozen wasteland!"

The Baron was working himself up into a towering rage, totally unlike either the frowning gloom or the smiling urbanity that Garth had seen heretofore, and the overman began to wonder if the man was sane. Surely such disparate moods were not quite normal in a single man!

"Well, I *have* ruled over this little trash heap of the gods. I have endured two dozen ten-month winters and as many muddy, malodorous summers, and I have had enough, more than enough! Other barons sneer at me. None have deigned to visit this pesthole for fear of contracting pneumonia, and when I have visited them I am seated at the foot of the table, like a commoner! Nor can I hope to improve my status by improving Skelleth, for there is nothing here to improve! The town was built as a frontier citadel for the Racial Wars, and has declined ever since. There is no money to be had here. I can afford no castle, no court; every cent of taxes is spent to maintain my three dozen guards, who are the laughingstock of every army in Eramma!"

The Baron had worked himself up into shouting, almost screaming. Now his voice dropped to a low and ominous tone.

"Listen, Garth, I have had enough. One way or another, I will change Skelleth or leave it. The next caravan will carry a letter from me to the High King, offering the services of myself and certain magicks in any war he chooses. If he ignores this, I will find my own use; with the basilisk I can take what I will. I can make myself King of Eramma if I want. If I give you the basilisk, I remain nothing, a worthless lord of an even more worthless land. Now, what compromise can you possibly suggest?" He glowered almost as balefully with his ice-blue eyes as Garth with his huge red ones.

The overman could think of no answer.

The Baron's anger subsided, and he seemed to collapse into himself, withdrawing into his gloomy silence again. It seemed to require an effort for him to order his men, "Take him."

The men behind the Baron surged forward and around him, but stopped just out of reach of Garth's sword; likewise, the men on the stair advanced, but did not attack, apparently unwilling to approach in such confined quarters.

Garth laughed, partly from genuine amusement at their timidity and partly to cow them further. He shifted his foot to his captive's neck, and announced, "I will slay this man after I have disposed of the rest of you, not before."

One of the men on the stairs gathered his courage and charged, yelling. Garth smashed at the attacker's hand with the flat of his broadsword, and sent the man's own weapon flying. The man, finding himself suddenly disarmed, turned his assault into a diving tackle. Garth caught him a blow on the head with the flat of the axe as he hit, so that the overman fell back against the wall while his assailant lay on the floor, stunned. Garth struggled for a few seconds to retain his balance and succeeded, stepping forward to straddle both the men on the floor, the one fully conscious and the other dazed. As soon as he did he found himself in combat, two short swords chopping at him. He dodged one and parried the other, and with a quick riposte ran the point of his blade through one man's shoulder. The guard gasped in agony and fell, writhing, as Garth withdrew the weapon just in time to counter another blow at his side. Holding the attacker's sword on his own, he brought up the axe in his left hand and hacked at the wrist behind the hilt. The soldier dropped his sword and fell back.

There was a momentary lull as others moved to replace their defeated comrades, and Garth took the opportunity to shout, "So far I have been merciful. The next man dies!"

The warning had an immediate effect, as the advancing men paused, uncertain.

"I do not wish to slay anyone, but neither do I wish to be defeated. Stand away!" As he spoke, Garth mentally congratulated himself upon having met his foes at a corner, where they could not approach en masse nor surround him. "Baron, this will avail you nothing except slaughter. Your men cannot take me!"

"Nor can you escape." The Baron's voice was quiet, barely audible, in contrast to Garth's shout, but its import more than made up for that, as the overman knew it was true. He could butcher anyone who approached him where he was, but if he moved out of the corner he would be surrounded and killed. Stalemate.

There was a sudden flurry of movement at the end of the corridor near the Baron. Someone had entered, and was whispering to his lord. Garth could make out nothing but the word "beast." He wondered what message could be arriving at such an hour and in such circumstances, but could do nothing to satisfy his curiosity. Instead he took the opportunity to kick away swords that had fallen within reach of the men he stood over, lest they retrieve and use them.

That done, he looked over the heads of the guards at the Baron's face. Whatever the news was, it seemed unwelcome, as the customary frown was deeper than ever. Then, with a curious shrug that seemed to leave him smaller than before and with an audible sigh, the frown vanished, to be replaced with an expression of utter despair such as Garth had seen heretofore only on caged animals—the expression that meant the animal would soon waste away and die. The Baron sagged, as if it took all his will merely to stand upright; he leaned heavily on the corridor wall.

One of the men-at-arms nearest the Baron asked solicitously, "Is there anything we can do, my lord?" His voice was sympathetic, but Garth thought he detected a note of contempt where he would have expected surprise or confusion. Surely this sort of collapse could not be a common occurrence?

The soldier had sheathed his sword and was helping the Baron to stand. He looked toward the overman, standing at the foot of the stairs on what would have been the natural route to the Baron's bedchamber, then glanced back toward the door to the dungeons, unsure which way to go. The messenger also looked about, apparently noticing Garth for the first time, and asked, "What should we do, my lord?"

The Baron shook his head and managed to croak, "Doesn't matter." Garth was appalled. The man was clearly suffering some sort of seizure, displaying the symptoms of a person in deep shock or sorely wounded. The entire party was now watching the Baron rather than the overman. Swords were lowered, crouches abandoned. Seeing the easing of tension, the man escorting the Baron led him through the cluster of soldiers, past the motionless overman, and up the stairs, where the remaining men fell back to make room.

When he was past and out of sight around the corner at the top of the stairs, a man remarked casually, "It's a bad one this time."

A companion nodded, as heads began to turn in Garth's direction again. The overman, for his part, was utterly astonished by this turn of events, and glanced about in confusion. Could this anticlimax be the end of the battle? He was about to ask what the messenger had told the Baron when he received an even greater surprise. The guardsmen on the stairs

moved abruptly downward, retreating from something, and there appeared at the top a huge black
catlike head, with golden eyes and gleaming fangs,
peering down at the torchlit corridor.

"Koros!" Garth's greeting burst forth involuntarily.
He was almost as amazed by how happy he was to see
the beast as he was by its presence. It growled pleasantly in response, but made no effort to move closer.
It apparently didn't care to try squeezing around the
corner onto the narrow staircase. Seeing this, Garth
ordered it, "Wait," and turned to the nearest guard,
one of those he had wounded in the brief melee.

"Where is the basilisk?"

"In the dungeon."

"Show me."

The man glanced around at his companions, who
merely shrugged or looked away. One ventured to
comment, "The Baron said it didn't matter." He did
not look as if he meant it.

Resignedly, the wounded man turned and led the
way to the door at the end of the corridor. Beyond it
was a small room holding a rough wooden table, with
several rings of keys hung on the wall and a statue
standing in the center. The statue was of a wretched
underfed youth. Garth stared at it in dismay.

His guide, feeling some explanation was in order,
said, "The Baron wanted to test the legend. He promised the boy his freedom if he lived."

"His freedom?"

"He was awaiting sentencing for theft."

"Oh." Garth paused as the man took a set of keys
from the wall and opened an iron-bound door at right
angles to the one by which they had entered. As it
swung wide to reveal a dreary stone passage, lit by a
single torch, he said, "Tell me about the Baron. What
is wrong with him, that he acted as he did just now?"

The man shrugged. "No one knows for sure. He's
always been that way. He has these moods every few
days where he refuses to do anything, he can't stand,
can't speak. Once or twice he has slashed his wrists,

but then bandaged them before the blood loss was serious. He's usually at his best, full of wit and charm, just a day or two before, which makes it seem all the worse. When he's well, he's a very clever man, there's no doubt, as methinks you've seen. But of late his fits have been getting worse. Some say he's under a curse, or that he deals with evil forces and suffers thus as payment."

Garth suggested, to see the man's reaction, "Perhaps he's mad."

"Oh, there's little doubt that he's mad! The only question is why."

This served only to confuse the overman. "If he's mad, why is he permitted to remain in power?"

The man gaped at Garth in astonishment. "He's the Baron! The High King gave Skelleth to his father! How could that be changed?"

Garth was on shaky ground, since he knew very little of Eramman politics, but ventured, "Could you not petition the High King to replace him?"

The man was slow in replying, "Well, I suppose we could. But why? He's not that bad, and he is our rightful lord. Better a madman like our own than one like the Baron of Sland!"

Since Garth had no idea who the Baron of Sland was nor what he was like, he could make no cogent reply. Instead he fell silent and permitted his escort to lead him into the passageway, a corridor about twenty feet long ending in another door identical to that he had just passed, with another corridor opening off the middle of the right-hand side and with several metal doors in the left wall, apparently leading to cells for imprisoning criminals. The smell of basilisk was readily noticeable.

The pair turned down the side corridor, which extended about thirty feet, with five doors on each side and a blank gray wall at the end, where another torch served to lessen the gloom. The guide stopped and pointed. "It's in the second cell on the left."

Garth nodded. "Where is the Sealing Rod?"

The man looked blank.

"The talisman that keeps it imprisoned. Where is it?"

He shrugged. "I don't know what you're talking about."

Garth, though annoyed, saw no reason for the man to lie. "Were you present when it was brought here?" he demanded.

"No."

"Well, fetch me someone who was."

The guard turned to go, and Garth suddenly realized what an incredibly stupid thing he was doing. It would be a very simple matter for the fellow just to close and lock the dungeon door and post guards with crossbows, in case Garth should hack down the door with his axe. Koros would be no problem; it had been told to wait, and as long as it was fed it would do just that. It might be a bit inconvenient having a warbeast in the front hall, but it could be lived with. And when Garth had starved to death, a way could be found to dispose of it.

"Wait!" Preferring safety to dignity, Garth ran to catch up.

# CHAPTER FIFTEEN

The gathering at the foot of the stairs had broken up. There was no sign of the recent abortive battle except one or two small spatters of blood on the stone floor. A lone guardsman sat on the bottom step, cleaning his sword. It was the man Garth had disarmed and knocked unconscious. His hand bore a few scratches where the rough hilt had been torn from his grasp. The sword was also scratched, apparently having suffered when so rudely flung about. As Garth and his escort approached the man picked it up to sight along the blade, and muttered, "Aghad and Bheleu!" The blade was bent.

The escort interrupted. "Saram, the overman is looking for someone who saw the basilisk put away."

The man addressed as Saram looked up and growled, "So what?"

"I don't know who was there. I thought you might."

"I was there myself. Why?" He looked from his fellow soldier to his recent adversary.

Garth spoke on his own behalf. "I want to know where the Sealing Rod is."

Saram squinted up at him, which Garth was sure could only be an affectation in the dim torchlight, and asked, "The what?"

"The wooden rod that keeps the basilisk caged."

"Is that what it is? A carved stick about thus?" He held up his hands to indicate the length, having laid his ruined sword on the step beside him.

"Yes."

"Why?"

"I want the basilisk."

"But why should I tell you?"

Garth had no ready answer.

"You're worried you won't get the monster out of here before the Baron comes out of it, eh? Probably right, unless you can make it worth my while to help."

Comprehension dawned on Garth. He dug out his purse and handed Saram a coin. Saram studied it, acknowledged it to be gold and of sufficient size, and stood up.

"I'll show you. Come along."

Garth hesitated, then ordered his original guide: "You too." Together they followed Saram as he stalked down the corridor, clutching his naked sword.

Having appropriated a ring of keys in the wardroom, Saram promptly went, not to the cell that held the basilisk, but to the last door on that side. Unlocking it at last after trying half a dozen different keys, he swung the heavy metal door open to reveal a tiny cell containing nothing but a mound of straw. He indicated the pile and said, "Under there."

Garth started to step into the cell, then thought better of it. That would be even stupider than merely getting himself locked in the dungeon. Grabbing the other soldier, he said, "You get it."

The man obeyed. Apparently no trickery had been planned. The rod was indeed under the straw, and was handed promptly to the overman.

"Good. Now unlock the cell with the basilisk in it."

Saram handed the keys to his comrade and said, "Here. Your turn." He then attempted a hasty departure, to be discouraged by the overman's hand on his shoulder.

"Wait. Don't look at it and you'll be safe." He motioned to the other, who reluctantly approached the cell he had earlier indicated, wrinkling his nose at the smell. The key turned in the lock, and the door swung out an inch.

Suddenly noticing that he was on the wrong side of the basilisk, Garth said, "Enough," and began walking up the corridor. The rod in his hand began to resist when he had gone a few paces, and he found it necessary to push it over toward the wall opposite the creature's cell; even then it required considerable force to move it, and he wondered how the Baron had ever gotten it there in the first place. Had the cell door not already been unlocked he might have dissolved the barrier, but as it was he did not dare, nor did he care to take the time to lock the door again for the few minutes necessary. Instead he merely pressed on, and heard a ferocious and familiar hissing in response. The two men-at-arms were rather visibly taken aback. It was only the fact that Garth had not yet sheathed his sword that kept the one whose name he didn't know from running.

Then suddenly he was past the crucial point, and the abrupt cessation of resistance almost sent him sprawling. Saram, his composure at least partly recovered, ventured, " 'Twas easier getting it in here."

Garth growled as he steadied himself, carefully looking away from that ominous inch-wide opening; his displeasure was caused as much by the dry, deathly stench that was filling the passage as by the man's irritating remark. The venomous vapor had had half a day to accumulate in the tiny room, and the air of that cell was undoubtedly lethal by now. Well, at least its next occupant need not worry about vermin.

He motioned for the guards to precede him out. He did not care to speak aloud and give that poisonous atmosphere greater access to his lungs. They obeyed promptly, both of them beginning to gag on the fumes. They had not developed the tolerance Garth had from his prolonged exposure in Mormoreth, and would probably have been more sensitive in any case, being merely human. They seemed too busy choking to try trapping Garth in the dungeon, but nonetheless he kept his sword ready and made sure both remained within easy reach until they were all in the wardroom. His left hand kept a secure hold on the rod, which he thrust into his belt.

There was a hiss from behind as the basilisk objected to being moved, and the nameless guard started to turn, thoughtlessly. Garth slapped him, hard, with the flat of the sword, leaving a small slash in the sleeve of his mail shirt where the edge had not been angled away sufficiently. Startled, the man looked at the overman rather than the basilisk. Without a word, Garth pointed at the petrified prisoner who stood a yard away. The guard shuddered and looked faint. Saram tried to grin, but he, too, was pale.

Since there were no further doors between him and the outside that could stand up to more than a few quick blows of his axe, he decided there was no reason to keep his two-man escort any longer. With a motion he indicated that they could go. The first promptly ran for the stairs; Saram started to depart at a more leisurely pace.

"Wait!" Garth called, remembering something. Saram stopped, but did not look back. Although, from where he was, the monster was around a corner and therefore invisible, he was not taking chances.

"Where is the cover for the enclosure?" Garth demanded.

Saram shrugged. "Don't know."

"Find it. You were there when the basilisk was delivered. You must have seen what became of it."

"It was dragged off toward the other stairs."

"Find it and bring it here."

Obviously none too pleased, Saram shrugged again, then nodded. He strolled off for the stairs again. Garth choked back an order to hurry; such a command would do no good when the man was out of sight. Besides, he was already beginning to regret opening his mouth at all. Though the vapors in the wardroom were not concentrated enough really to bother him, they seemed to have put a foul taste on his tongue that he would have greatly preferred to do without. He wondered whether the monster's trail would do any harm to his bare feet; it seemed unlikely, since it had only passed along this route once. In any case, he felt nothing but the ordinary cool stone against his soles.

Having sent Saram off, Garth now had to wait where he was, for fear of petrifying the guard on his return, should he move any further; this meant he had nothing to do but contemplate his surroundings and avoid looking behind himself.

There being little else in the room worthy of study, he found himself inspecting the remains of the unfortunate youth used to test the basilisk's legendary power. He was interested to notice the expression, which meant little to him, but was plainly not the look of abject terror he would have expected. He had seen human panic on Arner's face when that youth, somewhat older and a good bit healthier than the current specimen, awaited his execution, and the aspect of the alleged thief bore no resemblance to that distorted countenance. Instead, Garth decided, there was something resolved about it; the mouth was shut, even compressed, so that those hideous oversize human lips scarcely showed; the jaw was set and the eyes open, but not unnaturally wide. The overman found himself wondering what peculiar combination of emotions could produce such a look on the face of one facing certain death. No, not certain death; he had been told that he might die, or that he might go free. It suddenly struck Garth that the young thief had been inordinately brave to take such a risk. Theft was not a capital crime in Skelleth, he was sure. He did not know what the customary penalty was, but to gamble one's life, one's very existence, on an unknown chance for freedom, with no chance to defend oneself . . .

He shuddered slightly. It was not a thing he would care to do in such a situation. Though he thought highly of himself, Garth admitted that he probably would not have such courage. Perhaps the humans placed a higher value on freedom than overmen did, or a lower value on survival. The latter was certainly possible from what little he had seen of human society. Perhaps their beliefs in supernatural powers, gods and the like, had something to do with it; he had heard that most believed in some sort of existence after death, where the essence, the personality of the individual—they had a special word for it, the *soul*—lived on, in some other world. The idea seemed very nebulous and unlikely to Garth, but such a concept would undoubtedly account for the disregard for life some humans seemed to display—such as the dead thief he was studying.

But then, the boy had been very thin. Garth imagined he could make out the bones in his arms and legs, and ribs made visible ridges in his ragged tunic. Perhaps he had gone mad from hunger, like an unfed warbeast, and taken the first opportunity to leave his cell, despite the possible consequences. That did not explain what Garth was now fairly certain was the determined expression on the stone face, though; a starving warbeast appeared to be angry, enraged rather than determined.

Overmen, he knew, did not go mad from hunger— he had seen too many of his people starve to death in bad winters to doubt that—but perhaps humans did. He was musing on the Baron's apparent insanity, wondering if it were diet-related, when Saram called from the foot of the stairs. The villagers seemed to take their lord's insanity for granted. Such afflictions were plainly far more common among humans than among overmen.

It did not occur to Garth that his own behavior, leaving his home and family for an idiot quest after fame, might well be considered mad by his fellow overmen.

Turning his attention from such theoretical musings back to immediate concerns, he saw that Saram stood well down the corridor, facing the opposite direction and clutching a huge bundle of dirty cloth.

"Bring it here!" Garth called.

"Get it yourself," Saram retorted, dropping his burden to the floor with a rattle of chains.

Garth glanced down at the wooden rod at his belt,

then pulled it out and placed it carefully on the floor; he didn't care to haul the basilisk out into the passageway yet. Leaving the rod there, he strode down the corridor to where Saram stood, one foot on the bundle.

"It was in the armory," the guardsman said as Garth drew near. The overman suddenly realized that the man held a sword, not his ruined shortsword but a long, thin rapier that glinted where it caught the torchlight. Sometime during his wait, Garth had sheathed his own blade, and his hand now fell instinctively to its hilt.

"Oh?" Garth tried to sound noncommittal as he stopped a few paces from Saram's back. He had no idea what the soldier had in mind. Surely he could not plan to tackle an overman single-handed!

"It's a long trip to the armory."

Suddenly remembering Saram's earlier actions, Garth thought he understood part of the man's behavior, though the sword remained a mystery. He said "Oh" again, and pulled out a gold coin. An open palm appeared to accept it, apparently in response to the clink of metal when Garth reached into his purse. The overman put the coin on the palm, and both promptly disappeared. So did the sword, which was sheathed in the same flurry of motion.

"Anything else I can get you?" Saram still kept his back to the overman.

"No."

Saram shrugged, and strolled back up the stairs, leaving the cover where it lay on the floor. Garth watched him go, more than a little confused by the man's behavior. Had the sword been entirely to keep him from snatching up the cover without paying? It began to appear that all the humans he met were insane; the Forgotten King demanding delivery of a basilisk while swearing not to use it in the only way Garth could imagine, the Baron collapsing into a near-catatonic depression as he watched, the boy-thief risking his life for freedom, Saram's irrational behavior ... it was all more than Garth could understand.

Finally, shrugging, he turned and walked back to the wardroom, being careful not to look toward the basilisk. He untangled the cover as best he could in the limited space, then lifted it up to shield his eyes as he proceeded back into the dungeon. There was no room to drape it properly around the enclosure, so he made do with hanging it across the leading edge. There was barely room above the barrier to squeeze through enough chain and cloth to keep the battered shroud in place. Once that was done, it was a matter of a few minutes to drag the whole mess to the stairs and to start up them. There was some difficulty in getting the leading edge of the cover up the steps, and Garth found it necessary to feel his way back down, eyes closed, to untangle things three times.

A trace of venom had apparently found its way into the cut on his left foot and was stinging abominably, but Garth refused to let that slow him. Upon first reaching the top of the stairs, he saw bright morning sun pouring through a nearby window, plainly showing that it was full day out. He could ill afford to waste further time. The Baron might recover at any moment, or Herrenmer, the captain of the guard, might take charge and decide to stop the overman. Garth considered it fortunate that Herrenmer had not been present at the predawn encounter. Judging by his performance at the confiscation of the basilisk, he would not have allowed Garth to go on simply about his business as had the other guards.

As well as the sunlight, Koros was waiting at the top of the stairs. Garth greeted it affectionately, if rather hurriedly, and hooked the Sealing Rod into its halter before leading it out to the entry hall, carefully keeping the warbeast's golden eyes facing forward, away from the imperfectly hidden basilisk.

They met no one in the hallway. Undoubtedly the residents of the mansion didn't care to come too close to Koros' fangs.

In the entry hall two men-at-arms were guarding the front door, which stood slightly ajar. Garth could see splintered wood where lock and latch had been ripped out, presumably by the warbeast's entrance in pursuit of its master. The doors were still on their hinges, though, and reasonably intact. It was just as well. Garth had no wish to antagonize the Baron further, though he doubted that the mad nobleman would ever forgive what he had already done.

Upon seeing the overman and warbeast appear, the guards stepped back, and one drew his sword.

Garth said, "Don't worry; we're leaving. Shield your eyes; we are taking the basilisk."

The guards said nothing, but merely looked at one another, nodded, and stepped further back—through the door to the audience chamber. Garth continued forward and swung open the front door.

Immediately he regretted doing so. He reprimanded himself for not noticing the mutter of noise outside.

It was market-day, apparently; the square outside the mansion was thronged with people milling about, merchants hawking their wares, farmers selling their produce, and children running underfoot. Several turned and stared in astonishment at the armored apparition standing in the door of the Baronial mansion, and Garth stared back.

Offensive action seemed called for, before the crowd could remember its earlier aggression; Garth had no desire to be pelted with mud and stones again. He drew his sword and stepped forward into the sunlight, roaring at the crowd.

Immediately those nearest him fell back, terrified.

Koros, in response to its master's bellowing, appeared at his shoulder. The crowd's murmur died away for a long moment, then returned to a higher pitch. It occurred to the overman that he would have to empty the square completely before he could safely bring the basilisk out, since only in the square itself was there room to straighten the covering. Therefore he strode boldly forward with sword raised, his left hand unslinging his axe, the warbeast growling along a few paces behind him. When he had reached what seemed a good point, where Koros could join him without hauling the basilisk's enclosure past the open door of the mansion, he stepped up on a merchant's box and bellowed, "Go! This place is mine!"

Like magic, most of the mob evaporated. It had already cleared a wide path from the mansion door to his speaking-box, and that path quickly widened to include the whole square. Guards posted around the edge, whom Garth had not noticed before in the crowd, hesitated, but gave way before the rush of villagers and also retreated. A few die-hards remained, but another bellow and a swing of his sword sent them scurrying. A short charge and a feint in the direction of a straggler sent even the stubbornest fleeing. To be certain, Garth circled the market, bellowing and making threatening gestures up each street. The market-square was indeed empty.

Well satisfied with his achievement, Grath hurried to the basilisk's enclosure, as Koros dragged it forth, and rapidly spread the covering around it properly. He knew that any second people would begin drifting back to watch whatever happened. He only hoped that they would remain intimidated, and not work up a raging mob over his supposed responsibility for Arner's execution. He also hoped that the guards would not rally.

When the cloth-and-chain covering was securely in place, Garth tried to rush to Koros' side, but found himself limping badly on his injured and poisoned left foot, so that his progress across the square was more of a stagger than a run and his mounting more of a scramble than a leap. Once safely astride, he directed the warbeast toward the best route around the mansion toward the King's Inn, and looked at his foot.

The cut itself was insignificant, as he had thought all along, but the venom had caused massive swelling and discoloration. He comforted himself with the thought that there couldn't have been much of the poison or he would be dead already. As it was, he once again regretted the loss of his supplies; the medicinal herbs that now lay under a foot of rainwater could have treated the wound.

Also, of course, the warbeast's saddle would have been somewhat more comfortable than its bare back. That could be endured, however, though Garth would have preferred to have the guide-handle rather than merely the halter he had left on the beast.

To Garth's delight, the villagers fled before his advance. He had been rather worried that they might stand their ground. His extended contemplation of the petrified youth had given him a higher opinion of human courage than he had previously held.

Were it not for the pain in his foot, he would have enjoyed the ride; the sun was bright and warm, though clouds were gathering, and he was at long last about to deliver the basilisk to the Forgotten King. Unfortunately, the aching wound served to remind him of less pleasant matters; that he had lost all his supplies save a part of his gold, his sword, and his axe; that he had no boots nor cloak to his name; that he was surrounded by enemies; that the injury might well become gangrenous and therefore fatal; that he didn't know if the warbeast had found and eaten the goats. All in all, his situation struck him as unenviable, and he was very glad indeed that this ridiculous quest was nearing its conclusion. He had little patience left.

So little patience, in fact, that after installing Koros and the basilisk in the stable beside the tavern—and frightening away the new stable-boy—he marched boldly if somewhat limpingly into the King's Inn with drawn sword, ready to deal with whatever he might find there, up to and including the entire village guard. All he found, however, was half a dozen morning drinkers guzzling ale, the innkeeper polishing brass, and the Forgotten King sitting motionless at his usual table.

The overman stopped in the center of the taproom and looked around at the silent, terrified customers. A sudden feeling of anticlimax, like that following the

Baron's collapse, washed over him as he realized that this peaceful tavern was the end of his adventure. It seemed inappropriate. But then, he reminded himself, was this really the end? He had yet to deal with the Baron, and it might be some time before he could return again to his home and family. Also, there was still the mystery of what the Forgotten King wanted with the basilisk. He sheathed his sword, crossed to the old man's table, and seated himself.

The Forgotten King, as usual, did nothing to acknowledge his existence.

"I have brought the basilisk."

"Where?" The hideous voice was a shock, as always.

"In the stable, as you suggested."

"Good." The old man began to rise, but Garth caught his arm. He immediately regretted it; even through the voluminous yellow sleeve he could distinctly feel every bone and tendon, as hard and tense as wire. The arm had none of the natural warmth Garth had expected. He snatched his fingers back, as if burnt.

"Wait."

The old man seated himself again, his head raised, apparently looking at Garth, though his eyes were invisible under his hood.

"Will you tell me why you want the basilisk?"

"No." The voice seemed even drier than usual, and was definitely lower in pitch.

Garth thought better of further argument. After a brief pause, the Forgotten King rose, and this time the overman made no move to stop him. Instead he started to rise himself, only to sit down abruptly after attempting to put weight on his left foot. The old man gave no obvious sign that he had seen the movement, but he paused, standing beside the table, and hissed something in a language Garth had never heard before, totally unlike either the speech used throughout the northern lands or the ancient dead tongues the overman had seen in books. Then he turned and moved silently across to the door as Garth, somewhat taken aback, sat and watched him go.

It was only when the door had swung shut behind the tattered figure that Garth realized the pain in his foot was gone.

# CHAPTER SIXTEEN

By midafternoon Garth had given up wondering about the Forgotten King's purpose, and turned his thoughts instead to such practical matters as footwear. He did not care to go barefoot any longer than necessary; life without boots was proving thoroughly unpleasant. If his feet weren't being burned or stabbed, they were cold, or wet, or both, making his life miserable in any number of small ways. As the sunlight inched its way across the tavern floor, from early morning to noon, he had expected the old man's return at any moment and put off any real thought. As the bands of light beneath the windows swung past the vertical and began to lengthen, he had alternately worried lest the Forgotten King had accidentally perished and hoped that the old fool had indeed done so, all the while asking himself what use a basilisk could be. And now, as the light began to dim and the early diners arrived, he had turned to more worthwhile musings.

He had just decided that it would be perfectly reasonable to ask the innkeeper to recommend a good cobbler when the King at last reentered the taproom, as silent as ever but perhaps more stooped, as if dejected. Garth immediately surmised that whatever his goal might be, the old man had failed to attain it.

The yellow-robed figure slumped quietly into his usual chair, his head sunk low. Garth waited a polite moment before speaking, noticing that the ragged cloak the old man wore smelled faintly of basilisk venom.

"Greetings, O King."

183

The old man said nothing.

"What of the basilisk?"

"It lives." The dry voice was faint.

"What is to become of it now?"

"I care not."

"Has it served your purpose?"

There was a long pause, then what might have been a sigh. "No. No, it has not."

Before Garth could continue, something registered suddenly. For the past few seconds he had heard footsteps approaching the tavern, but had not paid any attention. A sudden realization catapulted that information to the conscious level and the center of his attention. The footsteps were those of several men, marching in step.

Soldiers!

There was a sudden blur of motion as the tavern door burst in, revealing a small crowd of the Baron's guards. Almost simultaneously, Garth jumped up and snatched up the heavy oaken table one-handed, to serve as a shield until he could draw his weapons. Two heavy crossbow quarrels thudded into the ancient tabletop, their barbed heads projecting from the solid wood in a direct line with Garth's chest.

Then, in shocking contrast to the flurry of activity, there was a long moment in which everything seemed frozen, suspended in time. Garth stood, his makeshift shield clutched in his left hand, his sword ready in his right, facing a dozen men-at-arms across half the width of the taproom. The crossbowmen seemed startled; they made no move to reload. The other guards were armed with swords—not their customary shortswords, but proper three-foot broadswords. The customers seemed paralyzed with astonishment, gaping at the battle tableau of a lone monster at bay holding off a dozen warriors.

And behind him, where the overman could not see him, the Forgotten King was grinning as he had not for centuries, his eye-sockets alight.

The silence was broken by a discordant screech from

behind the soldiers, barely recognizable as the Baron's voice.

"Kill him, you fools!"

Hesitantly, the foremost trio of guards advanced, only to fall back again as Garth crouched, sword raised. Again, all movement ceased, save for the maniacal dancing and yelling of the Baron, who stood in the doorway haranguing his men. The tension in the room mounted, as each side awaited a move from the other. Garth knew that his best move would be a sudden assault followed by a quick retreat, but he also knew that that would kill at least one of his foes, and he had hopes, even now, of avoiding bloodshed. He could see familiar faces among the guards. Herrenmer stood in the second rank, his steel helmet freshly polished; Saram held a crossbow and stood to one side, unmoving; the young man who had led him to the dungeon stood behind his captain; and other faces were also recognizable, men he had encountered upon his arrival in Skelleth, men who had saved him from the mob, men who had helped to confiscate the basilisk, men he had fought in the palace basement. Now they all stood facing him, with orders to kill.

Behind them the Baron continued to rave, his words all but unintelligible. Then one phrase suddenly rang out clearly in the tension-filled room.

"Remember Arner!"

Garth could see that those two words affected the guards, though he was not sure how. Expressions changed, stances shifted. Saram turned toward his master, his face showing surprise. Garth was too busy watching the swordsmen to pay much attention, until there came a sudden clatter.

Saram had flung down his crossbow. Even the Baron fell silent. Garth waited for the man to draw his sword, but instead he announced loudly, "This is stupid. Innkeeper!"

The other men forgot their opponent, and turned to gape in astonishment as Saram crossed to where the terrified tavernkeeper stood beside the huge casks.

"Pour me an ale, you old fool," said Saram in a normal voice that seemed like a bellow in the sudden stillness. The innkeeper hurried to comply, as Saram lounged comfortably against the wall and declared, "You people can get yourselves slaughtered if you want to, but I don't intend to die on behalf of a mad baron. Luck to you all!" With this last he raised his just-delivered mug in sarcastic salute, then gulped down a large mouthful of the foaming brew.

The guards looked at one another, dumbfounded. Then, abruptly, a man flung down his sword, saying, "Bheleu take it!" He, too, crossed to the liquor barrels and poured himself a drink, ignoring the protests of the innkeeper. That ended the tension, and in moments the entire party of soldiers was at ease, drinking, joking, and laughing. Only the Baron remained in the doorway, screaming imprecations at his men.

Garth relaxed, righted the table, and sat again, looking amusedly at the two shafts protruding from the wood. He was startled when Saram appeared, pulling up a chair.

"Mind if I join you?"

"Whatever you please. I am at your service." Garth was not given to polite exaggeration; he meant it. It was quite likely that Saram's disgusted revolt had saved his life, and he felt indebted to the man.

The guard casually took a long draught from his mug, and seated himself.

There came the noise of a commotion near the door, and all but the Forgotten King turned to see what was happening. The Baron, finally tiring of his ineffectual yelling, had snatched up a dropped sword, apparently planning to attack the overman single-handed. Several of his men had jumped him and were now struggling to get the weapon away from him before anyone was hurt. Garth could hear muffled curses from the writhing mass of men, and saw one man roll apart, his hand bleeding from a long, shallow scratch.

The man's voice rose above the hubbub. "Oh, Death,

that hurts! Aghad and Pria!" Several men not involved in the struggle rushed to his aid.

Then the knot around the Baron broke up. The sword had been flung safely out of reach, and the Baron lay on the floor, crying like an infant. With a low curse and a glance at his wounded companion, one man launched a vicious kick at the fallen noble's midsection. The Baron crumpled into a ball and lay sobbing.

Someone gently reprimanded the kicker. "You shouldn't have done that."

Herrenmer appeared from somewhere and knelt over his lord. Looking up, he called, "Someone help me; we'll get him safely in bed in the mansion." Willing hands reached out, and in a few moments Herrenmer and another guard were assisting the Baron, still weeping, out into the sunlit alley. The guard captain paused in the doorway to announce, "We'll be back soon."

The episode over, Garth and Saram turned back toward their table.

They sat silently for a moment as Saram poured his remaining ale down his throat. Then, thumping his mug on the table, he said, "I've been wondering about you."

Garth looked politely blank. "Oh?"

"Whatever under the gods brought you to Skelleth?"

The overman considered the question; ordinarily he would have refused to answer it, but in the present state of gratitude he felt unusually open and willing to talk.

"I was on a quest, of sorts."

"A quest?"

"Yes."

"A quest for what? I don't mean the basilisk; I mean why did you go off questing?"

"I wanted to do something of true significance."

"Go on."

"I wanted to change things, to have a lasting influence on the world. I went to an oracle near Ordunin, but was told that no mortal could change the way things are."

"Ah, so you asked to be immortal?"

Neither Saram nor Garth noticed the Forgotten King's reaction to this question; he looked up, light glinting in his eyes like two lonely stars in two black pits. Neither noticed, because Saram was too startled by Garth's reaction, and Garth was not noticing anything. Instead he was staring at Saram, his expression a baleful glare that appalled the man. For several seconds neither spoke. Then Garth muttered, "I never thought of that," and dropped his gaze to contemplate the tabletop.

There was another moment of silence, ending when Saram said, "Then what did you ask for?"

"I asked for fame—that my name be known forever."

"One of those!" Saram leaned back, studying the overman. "Why do you want fame? I never saw much point in it."

Garth looked up. "I wanted something to survive. I had never considered the possibility of living forever myself, but it seemed that having my name live on would be better than nothing."

Saram nodded sagely. "I see. Never thought that, myself, but I can see how one could. So you set out to become famous?"

"I asked the oracle how I might achieve everlasting fame."

"Oh?"

"Yes. I was told to come to Skelleth, find the Forgotten King, and serve him without fail."

"Find who?"

"The Forgotten King." Garth pointed a thumb at the old man, whose head had sunk back to its usual droop.

Saram's surprise was evident. "The old man?"

"Yes."

"Forgotten King? King of what?"

Garth shrugged.

Saram turned to the yellow-robed figure and demanded, "King of what?"

"Of Carcosa. In exile." The dry voice was quieter than usual, but still shockingly harsh.

"I never heard of it."

The old man said nothing, and Saram turned back toward the overman.

"Serving him was supposed to ensure eternal fame?"

"Yes."

"It seems unlikely."

Garth shrugged. "It was the word of the oracle."

"It still seems unlikely."

"I have reason to trust the wisdom and truth of the oracle."

"Well, I know nothing of that. But it doesn't seem possible. Nothing lasts forever, certainly not fame."

Garth shrugged.

"But think, Garth, can you name a single person who lived more than a thousand years ago?"

There was a sound that might have been a dry cough. But the Forgotten King was silent as Garth admitted, "No, but I have made no study of human history. Overmen have not existed that long."

"Well, can you name the first overman, or the wizard who created him?"

"No."

"Llarimuir the Great." Startled, both Garth and Saram turned toward the Forgotten King, who continued, "Llarimuir created a dozen overmen and overwomen simultaneously; there was no first."

Saram demanded, "How do you know that, old man?"

"I remember."

"But it was a thousand years ago!"

The Forgotten King said nothing, and after a moment Saram turned away again.

"Most people know nothing of that, and no one can say with certainty that this old fool is correct."

Garth said nothing. He was remembering the Forgotten King's eerie room upstairs and the casually miraculous cure worked on his wounded foot, and wondering who and what the King really was.

Undaunted, Saram continued, "How do you expect to achieve this fame? Do you expect the old man to tell you how? Or do you think he can do it for you?"

Garth remarked, quietly, "He is a wizard."

Saram snorted. "Then why does he live in a tavern in Skelleth? Why does he not have a place in the warm south?"

Garth shrugged again.

"So you intend to continue to blindly serve him?"

"I am not sure."

"Oh?"

"I am not sure I still want the fame I sought."

"Oh. But you still believe the old man could make it happen?"

"Yes."

Saram abruptly rose. "I'm going to get some more ale." He strode away, mail clinking faintly. Garth watched him go, then turned to the Forgotten King.

"You still will not say why you wanted the basilisk?"

The old man said nothing.

"Then what of my goal?"

"I have not yet decided upon your next task."

"Nor have I decided that I wish to accept it."

"What of your bargain?"

"I begin to doubt it."

"You doubt I can grant your desire?"

"No; I doubt whether I truly desire it, and at the price asked."

"Is the price too high?"

"It may be. It may be that I asked the Wise Women of Ordunin the wrong questions; it may also be that the deaths of a dozen men are more than I wish to pay."

"Yet, already, from this first errand, your name is known in Mormoreth and throughout Skelleth."

"Known as the name of a murderer!"

"Nonetheless, it is known. You made no provision as to how you wished to be remembered. You merely wished that your name be known until the end of the world, and I can promise that if you serve me successfully, you shall have that."

"I wanted fame, not notoriety!"

"You made no such specification."

Garth could feel a cold rage growing inside him. He felt betrayed, both by the Forgotten King and by the Wise Women who had sent him to Skelleth. He had trusted them; most particularly, he had trusted the King solely because the Wise Women had said he should, and trusted him to the point of killing for him. He said nothing, but merely glared at the ragged yellow cowl. Then, abruptly, he rose.

"Sit down."

The hideous voice could not be ignored; Garth hesitated, then sat, silent with fury.

"You would wish, then, not merely to have your name known, but to have it honored?"

Garth could not bring himself to speak; he nodded.

"I have no objection to altering our bargain to that effect."

His rage subsided in sudden confusion. "What?"

"You are from Ordunin."

"Yes." Garth was now completely bewildered.

"It is a poor city."

"Yes."

"Yet you have wealth. There is gold to be mined, fish in abundance, rich furs to be trapped. Why, then, are you poor?"

The overman made no reply at first. When the old man said nothing and the silence began to grow, Garth said, "Because we must trade away our wealth for food. An overman cannot live on fish alone, nor can every overman spend his time fishing, for someone must work the mines."

"Where do you trade?"

"At Lagur, ten days' sail southeast."

"Why?"

Comprehension was seeping in as Garth replied, "Because trade overland was impossible, we thought.

The Racial Wars made it so. And we know of no other ports."

As he spoke, Saram resumed his seat, a full mug sloshing in his hand. "What's due to the Racial Wars, did you say?"

Garth looked at the yellow-robed figure to see if he wished to explain and, seeing only a faint trace of a smile, said himself, "The impossibility of trade between Skelleth and Ordunin—and in fact, between all Eramma and all the Northern Waste."

"Well, the Racial Wars are long ended, it seems, yet there's still no trade, is there?" Saram gulped his ale. "I don't suppose Skelleth has anything you'd want up there. You've got ice and hay of your own."

"But you, here in Skelleth, can trade with the south."

"So?" Saram did not yet see Garth's point.

The Forgotten King interrupted before Garth could speak. "Saram, why is Skelleth dying?"

"Because we haven't got anything to eat or trade."

"And what if you had gold, and furs, and other valuable goods to trade with the south?"

Saram looked at the old man, then turned to Garth. "You mine gold up there?"

Garth nodded. For a moment the oddly assorted trio sat silently. Then the overman remarked, "There may be difficulties. They hate me here; I am blamed for Arner's death, and overmen are still mistrusted of old."

Saram waved that away. "No one will care once they see gold."

"I suppose not," Garth agreed.

The old man smiled sardonically, making his face even more horrifying than usual.

"Thus, O Garth, will you be known as the one to bring wealth and prosperity to Ordunin and Skelleth. Is this more pleasing to you?"

The Forgotten King's question needed no answer, but Garth had a question of his own.

"Why do you suggest this scheme? I have not fulfilled your purpose, you say, yet you offer this advice. Why?"

"Is it not to my benefit that Skelleth prosper? It seems now that I must live here for a time yet. I have no wish to inconvenience myself with either starvation or fleeing south, should Skelleth continue to decline."

There was a pause, then Garth replied, "Earlier you spoke of this being the age of decay, and told me that there was no way for mortals to defy the will of the gods and reverse that decay."

"Perhaps I was pessimistic."

The overman remained unconvinced. He said, after another moment's silence, "Whatever your reasons, the idea has merit."

"Indeed. So you will return to Skelleth with gold and furs, and become the hero and benefactor of its people. When you do, mayhap we will speak again."

"Perchance we will." Garth rose. "Though never again will I blindly obey you, O King. Saram, come. We have unfinished business."

Startled, Saram rose; not caring to argue, he followed as Garth led the way to the tavern door, pausing only to scoop up one of the two crossbows that lay where they had been dropped, motioning for Saram to get the other. He did, and followed Garth out into the alley, blinking in the slanting light of the setting sun as it peeped through the clouds. Though a few eyes glanced up curiously as the pair departed, the buzz of conversation did not lessen and no man moved to halt them.

Outside, the overman leaned his crossbow against the wall of the Inn and ordered, "Load them." He strode on and vanished into the stable. Saram shrugged and wound back the string of his weapon. He still wore a quiver holding eleven quarrels, not having bothered to remove it after the abortive battle in the tavern.

Inside the stable it was dim and cool, the pleasant smell of fresh hay and the stink of manure mingling weirdly with the stench of the basilisk. Garth crossed to where Koros stood waiting placidly, the Sealing Rod still securely tucked into its harness. A pace from the warbeast's side he stumbled over a small object.

Pausing, he looked down and saw he had trod on a stone, a curiously smooth and symmetrical stone. He picked it up, and found it was a stone rat; his foot had snapped off its tail, which lay in fragments amid the straw on the floor. He immediately turned his gaze to the other side of the stable, where the basilisk lurked silently within its enclosure. There was no opening in the cloth cover. The rat had not, then, chewed its way in; nor could it have crawled under the cloth, for how would it get back out, once petrified? No, the cover must have been lifted and replaced in the course of whatever the Forgotten King had done, and the unfortunate rat had been in line with the creature's gaze. Nothing else was disturbed. Odd that the King had taken such a risk as looking at the monster, Garth thought. Then he nodded slowly, before dismissing the matter from his mind and returning his attention to Koros.

When Garth emerged from the stable leading the warbeast, both crossbows were loaded and cocked, leaning against the wall. The overman picked up one in passing and Saram retrieved the other, following Garth at a distance of a few yards. They continued up the alley until the basilisk's enclosure appeared in the stable door and slid into the street. When it was clear of the doorframe and the cloth cover free of all snags, Garth stopped and pulled the Sealing Rod from its place in Koros' harness. Saram watched in some confusion as Garth proceeded to tap several of the carved facets, one after the other.

When he tapped the final spot, there was a soft sigh from the basilisk's direction, and Saram turned in time to see the cloth covering sinking to the ground, like a tent with its supports suddenly removed. It did not come to rest flat on the ground, but instead revealed the outline of an immense lizard, thrashing about angrily under the entangling fabric. Saram raised his crossbow.

Garth fired first; the bolt struck the basilisk in the neck, and the thrashing momentarily heightened as a gout of yellowish ichor stained the dirty cloth. Saram fired; his missile struck somewhere in the body, drawing another spurt of the basilisk's pale blood. The thrashing ceased as Garth calmly cranked back the bowstring for another shot.

He continued to wind, load, and shoot until all eleven quarrels protruded from the motionless form, and the alleyway reeked with the smell of basilisk more than it ever had with common ordure. A pool of reddish-gold, watery blood covered most of the fallen expanse of rough cloth, and a single green-scaled claw showed through a small tear. His last bolt shot, Garth thrust the now-useless crossbow at Saram, who accepted it while still clutching his own in his other hand.

The overman swung gracefully up onto the warbeast's back and announced, "You can tell the Baron that the basilisk is his, if he wants it. He can thank me when I return." Then, with a word to Koros, he rode off, turning north at the first corner and vanishing amid the first drops of a light rain.

# ABOUT THE AUTHOR

LAWRENCE WATT-EVANS was born and raised in eastern Massachusetts, the fourth of six children. Both parents were long-time science fiction readers, so from an early age he read and enjoyed a variety of speculative fiction. He also tried writing it, with little success, since he never finished a story.

Having survived twelve years of public school, he attempted to maintain family tradition by attending Princeton University, as his father and grandfather had done, but with rather less success than his forebears. After a year and a half of majoring in architecture, he flunked out as a result of too many parties and too few classes, and spent two years living in Pittsburgh (a city greatly underrated), trying to write for money and pretending to look for a real job.

At the end of this period he simultaneously sold his first story and was readmitted to Princeton. The story in question was one page of would-be humor; he returned to college, and got through two successful years, majoring in religion. Leaving once again on an indefinite leave of absence, which continues to this day, he married his high school sweetheart and settled in Lexington, Kentucky, where his wife had a job capable of supporting the newlyweds while he once again attempted to write. He also devoted considerable time to a hobby he had acquired three years earlier in Pittsburgh: collecting comic books. Thus it remains; he spends his days keeping house, buying and selling comics by mail, and writing. Since someone is reading this, plainly his writing has begun to pay off; within a year of moving to Kentucky he produced a full-length fantasy novel complete with ending and, to the astonishment of all, it sold.